THE ORIE CLARKE

CATHERINE DOBBS
DOTTIE SINCLAIR

Copyright © 2025 by Catherine Dobbs & Dottie Sinclair

All rights reserved.

No part of this book may be reproduced in any form or by any electronic or mechanical means, including information storage and retrieval systems, without written permission from the author, except for the use of brief quotations in a book review.

CHAPTER 1

1856

"Mama?" Jennie shuffled closer to her mother as the woman shivered beside her. "Are you cold?"

Mama gave her a smile that trembled. Her face was pale, and her lips looked a different colour.

"I'm…I'm fine, dear," she stammered. "It's just…just a draft."

"Are you sure, Mama?" Jennie sat up. "You can share my blanket. I don't mind."

"You keep it, Jennie. I'll be fine."

Jennie didn't believe that. She could tell that her mother was unwell, but she was refusing any help, trying to remain strong. Jennie didn't like the colour she was. It scared her.

The door opened, and her father shuffled into the room, coughing loudly as snowflakes fell from his shoulders and dropped onto the floor.

"Goodness, it's so cold out there," he said, slamming the door shut when it got stuck. "I thought I was going to struggle to get through the snow. It got thick out there."

"Is it bad?" Mama asked. "It looked fine this morning."

"More snow has fallen, I'm afraid." Papa took off his coat,

shaking it as he hung it up. "How are you feeling, darling? Any better?"

"Not bad," Mama replied, licking her dry lips. "I think I just need plenty of sleep."

Papa smiled softly as he walked across the room, leaning over to kiss his wife on the forehead. Jennie looked at her father and saw that he was of a similar colour to her mother. He didn't look well, either, and he was swaying on his feet. Worry gripped her chest.

"Are you all right, Papa?" she asked.

"I'm fine, sweetheart." He tapped her on the nose with his finger, a slight twinkle in his eye. "Have you been looking after your mother and brother today?"

"Yes. Stephen and I helped Mama with the washing, and we delivered it to the neighbours." Jennie looked towards the window. "Stephen said he was going to play with Edward outside a while ago."

"I saw him. He was trying to throw snowballs." Papa turned as the door opened. "Looks like it was too much for him."

"It's so cold!" Stephen declared, stomping the snow off his feet as he went over to the barely burning stove, holding his hands out. "I can't feel my fingers."

"That's my fault," Mama said faintly. "I was going to mend his gloves, but I didn't get the chance. I'll sort that out."

Jennie looked at her, knowing that it wouldn't be anytime soon. It had been over a week since Mama had fallen sick, and she had gotten worse in recent days. Her normally strong mother was fading before her eyes, and it was scary. Now she was curled up under a thin blanket on the bed the family shared, shaking to the point Jennie was surprised the bed wasn't moving.

She took her blanket and placed it over her mother before jumping off the bed, hugging her father.

"Do you want me to do anything, Papa?" She looked up at him. "You've been working all day."

"I'll be fine, honey." He kissed her head. "I'll see what there is for dinner. There won't be much, I'm afraid. Some bread and something warm to eat."

"It's fine. I'm not very hungry."

Even as she said it, Jennie could hear her stomach growling. The reality was she was starving, but she had gotten used to the hunger pangs every time it came to having a meal. They barely had any food to share between them, and her parents were already eating minimal amounts so their children could eat, but then Jennie would give her share to her brother and make sure Stephen had his fill. He was only four years old, and he was very vulnerable in this weather. Jennie knew it would break her mother's heart if her little boy died because he was malnourished.

Then again, they were all starving. Most of their money went to the rent, and they didn't have much for anything else. Jennie was aware of that after she heard her father having an argument with the big, scary landlord, who came by every week to collect the money. He kept putting the price up, and they were close to losing the one room they lived in.

Jennie overheard her parents talking about moving, but her mother was scared about ending up in the workhouse. Michael had assured her it wouldn't happen, but even he didn't sound convinced.

Jennie hoped things would get better once her mother and father recovered. Mama was unable to work as she could barely get out of bed, and Papa was working more shifts to fill in the gaps. He was exhausted, and Jennie occasionally accompanied her to the factory to help with cleaning the floors of the strands of wool that dropped from the looms. Once Stephen turned five, he would be joining in as well.

If only she got paid for it. Jennie knew she got nothing for helping, her father's employers seeing her as not important enough to get any money. She managed to get something from their neighbours when she and Mama did the washing for everyone, but it wasn't much. They were really struggling, and Jennie knew it was hurting her parents that it was happening.

She wished she was older so she could truly help. She couldn't wait to grow up.

"Why don't you get Stephen warm?" Papa suggested, nodding over at his son by the stove. "I'll make some food for you."

"But…"

"You are hungry, Jennie. Don't argue with me. You need your strength." He kissed her head. "I appreciate you saying otherwise, but you need to eat as well."

Jennie managed a smile and went over to Stephen, who was standing very close to the stove. Even though it didn't burn as brightly as it should, he was still going to get burned if he placed his hand on it.

"I'm so cold," he declared.

"I know." Jennie moved his hands away before he touched the metal and rubbed his hands between hers. "But you'll get warm soon."

"And I'm hungry."

"Papa is getting food for us. We'll be eating soon."

Jennie wished she could do more to comfort her brother. He was too young to understand any of this, that they were struggling. Then again, she was only six years old. She was not old enough for any of this, either, but she didn't seem to have much choice. Someone had to look after her mother while she was ill.

The sound of coughing from Mama made her look towards the bed. She was almost curled into a ball as she coughed, looking as if she was straining herself.

"Is Mama going to be all right?" Stephen asked with a whisper. "She's been sick for a long time."

"She'll be better soon," Jennie whispered back.

"When?"

Jennie wished she knew the answer to that. She squeezed her brother's hands and let go.

"Soon," she said.

She wished she knew the answer, but a part of her was pushing away the hope that things were going to get better. Especially with her mother coughing away in the background. That was enough to make her want to cry.

Deep down, she knew that Mama was not going to get better.

* * *

"COME ALONG, JENNIE," the matron said briskly. "Let's get inside."

Jennie looked up at the building before her. It was large and intimidating, towering over her and Stephen. It looked cold and isolating in the mid-February weather. Beside her, Stephen shivered and shifted closer to his sister.

Jennie wanted to cry as well. This was not how things were meant to go. She and Stephen were supposed to be with her parents, and they were meant to be living together. Now her parents were gone, and they were being put in the orphanage. Jennie had seen the building itself whenever she accompanied her father to the factory, and it looked like it was full of ghosts. It made her want to run away.

Now she had no choice as she had to go into it. She could feel her heart beating so fast it was making her breathe fast. She wanted to be sick, a nasty taste filling her mouth.

"I'm scared, Jennie," Stephen said, clutching onto her hand. "I don't want to go in."

The matron sighed and shook her head.

"I'm afraid you're going to have to go in, Stephen. You two will be out on the streets, and we can't have that."

"We'd rather be on the streets," Jennie declared defiantly. "We want to be back with Mama and Papa."

A look of sympathy passed across the woman's face, but it was only for a moment, and she grabbed Jennie's hand.

"Let's get inside."

Jennie wanted to pull away, but the matron was too strong. Her brother squealed and held onto her other hand tighter, both being pulled along. Jennie felt tears streaming down her cheeks, and she wanted to fight and scream. She was tempted to bite the woman and scratch at her, even if it made her look feral.

This wasn't what she wanted. She wanted her parents back. But after waking up a few days ago and finding Mama dead beside her, ice cold and clinging to herself, that life began to fade away. And it soon became impossible when, just a week later, Papa's sickness got worse and he died as well, collapsing in the street and freezing in an alley.

Jennie could still remember waking up by the stove, where she and Stephen had curled up with a blanket, to find her mother frozen in the bed, and then when Papa died, and a neighbour told them what happened. Only a couple of weeks after they both fell sick, they were gone.

Her throat was still sore from all the crying. This had to be a bad dream, but every time she closed her eyes, she saw their still bodies, felt the cold in the room. Jennie remembered touching her mother's arm and feeling how stiff she was.

At least Stephen hadn't seen that, although Jennie wished someone else had told him about their parents. The screaming when Stephen refused to believe her still rang in her ears.

Now her own screaming was echoing around her head as the matron pulled them into the orphanage.

"What is this racket?" A woman came out of a room off the main foyer, frowning at the group of three. "Miss Rupert, what's going on?"

"It's the Clarke children, Miss Maidstone," Miss Rupert gasped, her face red in her exertion. "They're being petulant."

"We want Mama and Papa!" Stephen cried, pulling on Jennie's arm until she felt like she was being pulled in different directions, and that made her scream louder. Miss Maidstone sighed and hurried over, lifting Stephen up and making him let go of Jennie.

"For goodness' sake, would you stop it? Your sister isn't a doll. Miss Rupert, would you take this one to the other children? I've got someone here to see the girl."

Jennie was confused. Someone was here to see her. How did anyone know that she was here already? Was it a family member she didn't know about? If that was the case, why would they only want to see her and not her brother as well?

"Jennie!" Stephen screamed as Miss Rupert let go of her hand and took him from Miss Maidstone. He reached for her. "Jennie, help!"

"Stephen!"

But Miss Maidstone gripped onto her shoulders and kept her still as he was carried away. Jennie could only watch helplessly as this happened, feeling her heart breaking into several pieces.

"He'll be all right, Jennie," the woman assured her, taking her hand. "Come on, there's someone to see you."

"I don't want to."

Miss Maidstone sighed and tugged her along. Jennie tried to make her stop, but she wasn't strong enough to pull away. They entered a large, plain-looking room with sparse furniture. A man was standing by the window, looking out into the desolate yard beyond. He turned as they came in, and Jennie found herself shrinking back. She didn't like the look of him. Tall, fair-haired with a beard, he looked like a giant from one of the stories her mother used to tell. His clothes were nice, indicating that he had some money and took care of himself. His blue eyes took Jennie in, and he arched an eyebrow.

"Is this one of the girls?"

"She's just arrived. I remembered what you said you were looking for, and she should be just right for what you want."

Jennie looked up at Miss Maidstone. What was she talking about? The man approached her, leaning over and making her shrink back.

"How old is she?" he asked as if she couldn't speak.

"She's six."

He pursed his lips, tilting his head and looking her up and down. Jennie wanted to cling onto Miss Maidstone's hand, but she didn't want to be holding onto her, either.

"What's your name?"

This was directed at her. Jennie didn't want to answer; he scared her too much.

"Jennie Clarke."

"Do you think you're a hard worker, Jennie?"

"Of course." She lifted her chin. "My parents always said so."

He grunted and straightened up.

"There's a spirit in her. I like that." He nodded at Miss Maidstone. "I think she would be just right for what I want. We're short of wool scavengers, and I think she would be ideal."

"That's good," Miss Maidstone said, sounding pleased. "How many more children would you need?"

"About half a dozen. The more, the better. Six to eight years old is preferable. They're just the right age to concentrate but not too big that they can't get under the machines."

Jennie had no idea what they were talking about for a moment. Then she realised they were talking about putting her to work in a factory.

"Where am I going?" she asked.

"Mr Cooper is going to take you to a place called Guildford," Miss Maidstone said. "It's outside London. You're going to be working in a cotton mill."

"What about my brother? Is he coming as well?"

Miss Maidstone glanced at Mr Cooper, whose mouth twitched a little. Jennie wondered what he found so amusing about what she asked.

"Once he's old enough, he can come and join you."

"Why not now?"

"Because he's too young, and I don't want to be responsible for a smaller child."

Jennie panicked again. Were they going to separate them? She shook her head and tried to back away, but Miss Maidstone pulled her back, causing her to stumble.

"I don't want to go anywhere without my brother," she said firmly. "Stephen comes with me, or I don't go at all."

"Do you think you're in a position to bargain with me for that, Jennie?"

"What does that mean?"

Mr Cooper crouched down, looking at her with those eyes that made Jennie shiver. She had heard from her mother that there were people who had cruel eyes, and she hadn't believed it at the time. That couldn't be possible. But now she understood what she meant. Mr Cooper had cruel eyes. Which meant he wasn't a good person.

"Your brother is too young to come with you. I can't have him at the factory as he could get hurt. But once he's old enough, he can join you at the mill. Is that fair enough?"

Jennie wasn't sure if she believed him. He looked sincere enough, but Jennie felt uncomfortable. She gulped.

"Do you promise?" she asked. "I don't want to be apart from my brother."

"I promise."

Jennie remembered something her father had done when he was making a promise. He held out her hand, and Mr Cooper looked at it in surprise.

"What are you doing?"

"When you make a promise, you shake on it," she said clearly. "Papa said honest people don't mind shaking hands if they've made a promise."

He looked bewildered, but he gently took her hand and shook it, regarding her curiously.

"You're an interesting child, Jennie Clarke," he murmured. "I can see you're going to be a...contributor."

"What does that mean?"

He didn't answer her. Instead, he got to his feet and turned to Miss Maidstone.

"I'll take her with me now," he said briskly. "I've got to get back to the mill, so round up a few more of the children."

"Can I see my brother first?" Jennie looked at the woman beside her. "I want to see him."

Miss Maidstone looked like she wanted to argue but instead huffed in response with a nod. Then she left the room, and Jennie felt the cold wrap around her again.

She had a feeling that things were not going to get any easier.

CHAPTER 2

The last memory she had of her brother was still in Jennie's head even after they had left London behind and were making their way along the winding roads. Stephen had been crying, clinging onto her as she was pulled away. He kept reaching for her even as he was carried out of the room, tears streaming down his cheeks. Jennie's face was still wet from her own torrent of tears.

She couldn't believe this is what had happened. Not too long ago, she had lost both of her parents within days of each other, leaving only her and Stephen. No other family had come forward to claim them and take them to a home, so they were taken to the orphanage, only to be separated as soon as they arrived.

It felt like this was the plan from the beginning. Why couldn't they stay together? Jennie wanted to fight and kick back, demanding to have Stephen come as well. But Mr Cooper had promised her he would join her soon once he was old enough. She was going to hold onto that promise.

Nobody decent would break a promise. Her father had taught her that.

They finally arrived at the mill, which was at the top of a hill surrounded by trees. The town of Guildford was in the distance, smoke coming from other factories dotted around. Guildford itself looked like a busy place, and the mill looked down on it all.

There was something a little scary and foreboding about it, and Jennie felt a chill that wasn't from the cold run down her back as she looked out of the window at it.

Was this to be her home from now on? How long would she have to be here before she was allowed to go back to Stephen? Would Stephen still remember her?

She didn't want to think about that, or she would start crying again.

The carriage pulled up at the entrance of the mill. There was a grand-looking manor house nearby, the windows looking so big Jennie was surprised it wasn't completely made from glass. As she climbed out, the door opened and a boy about eight years of age came out. He ran over to Mr Cooper as he alighted from the carriage with a beaming smile.

"Pa!"

"Maurice." Mr Cooper stopped him from hugging him, ruffling the boy's hair with a slight smile. "Have you finished your lessons for the day?"

"Yes, Pa," Maurice said eagerly. "I even completed my sums."

"Good boy."

"Are you coming inside? I want to show you what I've been reading."

Jennie felt a pang of jealousy as she saw this boy looking up at Mr Cooper with obvious adoration. She had once had that with her own father, but now he was gone. She would never be able to experience the same thing again.

Tears pricked at her eyes again, and she sniffed, wiping her nose with her sleeve. That was when Maurice noticed her, and he stared at her.

"Why are you crying?" he asked.

"She's just had a long journey," Mr Cooper said before Jennie could open her mouth. "Go back inside and get Mr Lewis to listen to you reading. I've got to get this one settled in."

"I see." Something shifted in the boy's face, and his smile faded. "Yes, Pa."

Jennie felt guilty. She was pulling this man away from his son, and she didn't want to get in the way. She bit her lip.

"I'm sorry," she mumbled.

Maurice frowned.

"What for?"

"For taking your father away."

Maurice looked surprised at that. His mouth opened and closed, blinking at her with a perplexed expression.

"I...it's fine," he stuttered. "He's always busy."

"At least one person here understands," Mr Cooper grunted. "Go back to Mr Lewis, Maurice. Come along, Jennie."

He took Jennie's wrist and tugged her towards a simple red brick building alongside the mill. She looked back and saw Maurice watching them, a sad look on his face. It was clear that he wanted his father's attention, but Mr Cooper didn't care to give that to him. He was more focused on his business than his own child.

She tried to give him a smile, but she was pulled along and nearly lost her balance. They entered the building and went up a set of stairs. Mr Cooper reached the first door and opened it. A large woman with wispy brown hair tucked under a cap was making a load of small beds.

There were at least a dozen beds in such a small room, and they looked like they barely fit one person on them. She was tugging the sheets off and placing them in the basket by her feet.

"I've got a new addition for you, Mrs Dobson," Mr Cooper said, pushing Jennie forward. "I've got a few more coming in the next couple of days, but here's one for now."

Mrs Dobson looked Jennie up and down with a critical eye, and she sniffed. She didn't look particularly happy to see her.

"She looks like a tiny thing. Do you think she'll be able to cope with the work?"

"Absolutely." Mr Cooper sounded confident. "She's tougher than you think."

Jennie shivered as the woman stepped towards her, making her feel even smaller as she craned her head back. Mrs Dobson's lip curled.

"She looked like she isn't capable of doing anything."

"Trust me, she'll be perfect for the scavenging. But, for now, I want her to help you with the housekeeping until we get her settled."

Mrs Dobson didn't look thrilled at the idea, and Jennie was hoping she wouldn't be left alone with her. She was frightening. But then the woman turned away, pointing at a larger basket across the room.

"Get the sheets out and start putting them on the beds," she barked. "And be quick about it."

Jennie wanted to say that she had no idea how to make a bed, but she was scared that she would be punished if she said so. Hurrying over to the basket, which was almost bigger than her, she tugged at a sheet, which almost toppled the basket over. Jennie caught it before it fell, straining to put it back to where it was. Then she went over to the nearest bed, trying not to look at anyone.

"She's obedient," Mrs Dobson grunted. "I'll give her that. That's something."

"She's got a bit of fire in her, but you won't have to worry about that. You just whip her into shape, so to speak."

Jennie tried not to tremble when she heard that. She didn't like the sound of that remark. Did they beat people here?

She couldn't stay here, but what choice did she have? They were in the middle of nowhere, and Jennie had never been to the town of Guildford. If she tried to escape and leave, she wouldn't know who to ask for help or where to go. It was a chilling thought.

She looked towards the window, wondering what Stephen was doing and if Miss Maidstone was looking after him. The woman who ran the orphanage had been rather reluctant to respond to Jennie's begging, but she had promised to make sure he was cared for.

Jennie couldn't wait to see Stephen again.

"Let's leave her to it, Mrs Dobson," Mr Cooper said. "I'm sure the beds will be made in no time."

"Are you sure, sir? She looks a little sluggish."

"Oh, she'll be fine. If it isn't, you know what to do."

The two of them left, and Jennie's heart sank, her stomach churning. They were going to punish her if she got this wrong. She didn't want to do it anymore in case they did do that.

She sank onto her knees and started to sob, burying her face into her sheet.

* * *

She managed to get the beds made and, to her surprise, Mrs Dobson thought she did a decent job. She gave Jennie a few pointers on how to make it better, but she left it alone. Jennie was glad about that; she couldn't bear to think she had done it wrong and would get beaten for it.

Dinner was not long after, and Jennie was led into the dining room, which was basically a long line up to a table that had a large cauldron on top. Mrs Dobson stood beside it with a ladle, and the children approached her with a bowl. She scooped out something cream coloured from the pot and dropped it into the bowl. The children bowed their heads and then left.

Jennie wondered what the food was. She couldn't imagine it was anything nice. But then her stomach growled, and she was reminded that she couldn't remember the last time she had eaten anything. She would probably eat whatever was put in front of her, if only to keep her stomach quiet and push the hunger pangs away.

She moved into the line behind a boy and a girl who had significant height differences. The girl was almost a head taller than Jennie while the boy was her size, but both were very thin. And the boy was swaying a little on his feet. Jennie didn't need to look at his face to know he wasn't well.

The girl looked around, surprised to see someone behind her, and gave her a smile.

"Are you new?" she asked.

Her accent was thick, one that Jennie hadn't heard before. But it was nice to listen to. She nodded shyly.

"Yes."

"What's your name?"

"Jennie."

The girl nudged the boy beside her to get his attention.

"My name's Polly, and this little one is William. Say hello, William."

William mumbled something, giving Jennie a shy smile before turning away. He did look very pale, and Jennie was surprised he was still upright. Polly sighed and shifted back to stand beside her, brushing her flaxen hair out of her face.

"He's not been well over the winter. Even a spell in the infirmary didn't make him feel better."

"What's wrong with him?" Jennie whispered.

"Nobody would tell us. We think it's consumption. It's normal to fall sick here, sadly."

Jennie's stomach clenched, and she felt like she was going to be sick. She took a deep breath and absently dusted down her dress.

"What is it like working here?" she asked. "Is it difficult?"

"You've not worked in a mill, have you?"

"I helped my Papa at his factory, but…he died…"

Saying that brought more tears to Jennie's eyes. She didn't want to start crying now. Polly gave her a sympathetic smile.

"It's not easy to handle something like that. I lost my parents when I was three. I'm nine now, and I've known the orphanage or the mill ever since. But a day doesn't go by where I don't miss them."

"Does it go away?" Jennie asked timidly.

"Not really, but you get the hang of handling it. Eventually." Polly reached out and touched Jennie's shoulder. "It's going to be raw for a while. Mrs Dobson says that you must get used to it. No one is going to give you any sympathy because you lost someone."

Jennie didn't like hearing that. She just wanted to sob in someone's arms and wish for her parents back. She could still remember the last time she hugged them, just before she and Stephen fell asleep. Her mother had been coughing violently in bed, but she managed to ease off enough to fold Jennie into her arms for a moment before kissing her head. Then Father kissed her cheek and told her to be a brave girl. They both said that they loved her and Stephen, and she needed to watch over her brother.

And the next morning they were gone.

Did they know they were going to die? Was that why they said all of that? Jennie felt like she had failed them already, given she had already been separated from Stephen. She could still imagine him crying for her back in London, wailing for her to return.

Mr Cooper had made a promise to her, and Jennie was going to hold him to it.

They reached the front of the line, and Polly handed Jennie and William their bowls from the table.

"Don't give Mrs Dobson any back talk," she whispered. "She's always in a bad mood, and she won't appreciate someone saying her food tastes bad."

"Does it always taste bad?" Jennie whispered back.

Polly made a face before she had her bowl filled by the large woman. Mrs Dobson did the same with William's before dropping whatever lumpy mush was in the ladle into Jennie's bowl. The smell made Jennie unsure whether to be ravenous or nauseous.

"Get some bread from the other table," Mrs Dobson said sharply. "And don't sit around talking. There are lots of things you need to do."

Jennie didn't know how to respond. She just followed Polly and copied her before sitting next to her at the end of a long table. William sat across from them, picking up a spoon and beginning to eat. Jennie peered at the mess in her bowl.

"What is this?"

"It's meant to be porridge or something. But the texture of it gets worse the further back in the line you are." Polly dipped her spoon into the sludge. "It doesn't taste too bad if you imagine it as something else. But when you're hungry, you don't get to complain when there's no other option."

Jennie grimaced, picking up her spoon. She got some out of the bowl, trying not to inhale, and stuck the spoon into her mouth. Polly was right that it didn't taste too bad, but it was very thick. Jennie managed to swallow it down.

At least it was something. She needed to eat at some point. Trying to imagine it was her mother's stew, Jennie managed to eat it all, wolfing down the stale bread. Polly gave her a smile.

"That's it. You've got it."

"I'm so hungry." Jennie finished her mouthful. "Do you think I could have some more?"

William giggled.

"You ask that, and you'll be in trouble. We're not allowed to ask for more, even if we're very hungry."

"Nobody wants more of that slop, anyway." Polly wrinkled

her nose. "We must eat it because we have no choice. To go and get some more is ridiculous."

"I'm just so hungry," Jennie said quietly, looking down at her empty bowl. "I haven't eaten properly in a long time. I wanted to make sure my brother ate so he took more of my food."

Now she couldn't do that, not when they were apart. She started to cry again, but she tried to keep the tears back. It made her embarrassed to cry in front of everyone in the room. Polly switched their bowls, patting Jennie on the back.

"You have mine, then. I'll be fine with just the bread."

"I…"

"You're so thin, and I can tell you're starving. You're going to need your strength to be here, and you can't start like you are." Polly smiled. "But if you stick with me, I'll look after you."

"And me," William piped up. "I'll look after you, too."

Jennie wanted to cry more hearing that. The only people she had to rely on when she was back in London were her parents. She had had a few friends, but things had happened so fast that she didn't get a chance to say goodbye to them. And these two children, who didn't know her, were willing to look after her regardless.

"Thank you," she mumbled.

"You don't need to thank us. Not yet anyway." Polly nudged her. "Just keep your head down and work hard, and you'll get through this a lot easier. Although it's not an easy stay when you're being made to work for nothing, but it's less taxing if you work."

"And if you show you've got a talent for something, you might be lucky and get a good job here," William added. "If you don't, you're stuck as a mule scavenger under the cotton machines until you're too old to get under there."

Jennie let all this sink in as she ate her second bowl of gruel. She didn't like the sound of any of this, but she didn't have a choice in it.

Like it or not, she was stuck here.

CHAPTER 3

1858

"What are you doing out here, Jennie?"

Jennie gasped and jumped to her feet, dropping the book in her hands. It bounced on the slabs and some of the pages slid away, fluttering in the wind. Mr Lewis, the schoolteacher, had rounded the corner and was watching her curiously. Jennie's face felt warm, and she blinked back her tears as fear gripped her throat.

She had been trying so hard not to get caught, and now she was going to get punished.

"Jennie?" Mr Lewis peered at her. "Why are you here?"

"I..."

Then he spied the book on the ground and crouched down. Jennie held her breath as he gathered the scattered pages, slotting them back into the book before standing up and looking at the title.

"*Frankenstein*. It's a bit complicated for you, isn't it?"

"Polly found the book a while ago, and she said it was really good." Jennie bit her lip. "My reading is not good, so I thought I'd practise with this book to make it better. I didn't mean to do anything bad…"

"I never said you did. I'm just surprised that you wanted to sneak away from your work to read. And that nobody's said you're missing."

"I was told I would be covered if anyone asked."

Jennie wasn't about to drop her friends in it. Polly and William knew she was self-conscious about her struggles with reading and writing, and they urged her to practise elsewhere so she could keep up. Jennie felt bad for leaving them with her work while she was trying to do her schoolwork, but she appreciated it.

"I'm just struggling in class, Mr Lewis," Jennie went on, feeling like she needed to fill the air as the man stared at her. "I'm getting fed up with the other children laughing at me because I don't understand something. I want to keep up and know what's going on, but it's hard."

"Why didn't you come to me? I would have listened."

Jennie looked at the ground, shuffling from foot to foot. She found the men and women around the mill intimidating. They were very strict. Mr Lewis was the kindest of the lot, but he was still someone she couldn't approach.

"I'm scared," she whispered.

"Scared of what?"

Jennie didn't answer. Mr Lewis sighed and pushed his spectacles up his nose before scratching his bald head.

"Well, I know you're behind on your lessons, so asking for you to have an extra few sessions to catch up shouldn't be too much of a problem…"

"I don't think Mr Cooper is going to like it," Jennie pointed out. "He's going to be upset when he finds out I'm sneaking away to read instead of work."

"I think that should be the least of your worries, but you have a point there." Mr Lewis opened the book and started putting the pages in the right order. "We're just going to have to be sneaky about it, then, aren't we?"

"Mr Lewis?"

"I am more than happy to give you lessons in secret, although it will mean making sure nobody else finds out about them. Mr Cooper will certainly not be happy once he finds out, but I can't bring myself to walk away when you really need help."

Jennie thought she was hearing things. She had thought the schoolteacher would tell her off and send her on her way before telling Mr Cooper about her neglecting her duties. Instead, he was offering to teach her in secret. This couldn't be happening.

"Are you sure about this?" she asked nervously. "I don't want to get you into trouble as well."

He smiled, his eyes twinkling behind his glasses.

"You don't have to worry about me. I'm more interested in helping my charges."

"But you're just the schoolteacher."

"I'm glad you've noticed that about me," he said dryly. "But I'm dedicated to my job, and if someone's showing that they want to learn further, it's up to me to make sure they can get better."

Jennie managed a smile. At least he wasn't mocking her for attempting to read something beyond what she was capable of. *Frankenstein* was complicated to read, and she hadn't understood most of the words. To have Mr Lewis say he would teach her made her feel better.

Reading anything was better than being told to sit down and do nothing in her free time. Which wasn't much when they had to work all day with a couple of hours off to have their lessons. Even then, not much was learned when the children often didn't want to be taught and wanted to just play. Jennie sat at the back with Polly and William, trying to keep her head down and get on with everything. But that somehow made her a target.

Some of the other children thought she was a strange girl, so she ended up having several mean comments thrown in her direction. Apart from Polly and William, it was hard to make friends.

"How long have you been here now, Jennie?" Mr Lewis asked suddenly.

"I…" Jennie frowned. "I was six when I came here. I'm now eight."

"So you've been at the mill for two years."

"Yes, and I'm hoping to see my brother soon."

"Your brother?"

"Stephen." Jennie's heart lightened as she thought about her little brother. "He's going to be six now. Mr Cooper promised that he would bring him to the mill as well so we could be together once he was old enough. Do you think he'll be here soon?"

She saw a flicker behind Mr Lewis' eyes, and he glanced away with an awkward expression. Jennie felt a trickle of trepidation down her spine. What did that mean? Did he know something?

"Mr Lewis?"

"I don't think you should worry too much about your brother, Jennie."

"Why not?" Tension gripped her stomach. "Nothing's happened to him, has it?"

"No, that's not it." He cleared his throat. "I mean, I haven't heard anything about any new arrivals coming here, and Mr Cooper keeps all the staff up to date with it so we can prepare. He's not mentioned anything about your brother."

"But…he promised! We shook hands." Jennie looked at her hands, remembering that moment clearly. "Papa said anyone who broke a promise after a handshake was not a good person. And Mr Cooper looked me in the eye when he said it."

"I'm sorry."

Did that mean she had been holding onto false hope all this time? Jennie's hands began to shake. She recalled what she said, and she knew what Mr Cooper had said. Stephen should be with her by now. They were meant to be together. How could she keep her promise to her parents about looking after Stephen if they were apart?

Her chest tightened, and she found herself struggling to breathe. Mr Lewis' expression turned into one of pity and he touched her shoulder.

"I'm sorry, Jennie. I think you must accept that Stephen is not coming here. If he is, it won't be soon."

"But he promised..." Jennie whispered.

"I'm afraid there are people in life that you can't trust to keep what they say to you as something to follow through on."

"And Mr Cooper is someone I can't trust."

Mr Lewis sighed, but he didn't answer. He didn't need to, though; Jennie knew what he was thinking.

Mr Cooper had lied to her. He was going to leave her on her own without her brother. And Jennie felt more alone than she had before.

* * *

"What are you doing here?"

Jennie looked up. Maurice was standing in the doorway of the clock room, watching her curiously. Jennie wiped at her face and moved to hide the book.

"I'm just sitting here," she said stiffly.

"On your own?"

"We never get a chance to be on our own, Maurice. I just wanted to get away from everyone."

This was the closest Jennie could have gotten to running away. She wanted to, but she was too scared to go beyond the edge of the grounds. So she scuttled up the little clocktower further down the hill, just to get away. It was where she went after being caught by Mr Lewis.

She didn't want him to see that she was still miserable even a week after being told that she would not get what she had been hoping for.

"Why here, though?" Maurice asked, watching her in confusion.

"Because it's quiet." Jennie glared at him. "You're not going to tell your father where I am, are you?"

He shook his head.

"No, I wanted to get away from him, too. Although he probably wouldn't notice if I was gone."

"Why not?"

Jennie was genuinely curious about that. As far as she was aware, Mr Cooper acknowledged his son and wife, keeping them in a good house with better food than whether everyone at the mill was being given. The children were treated worse than the grown men and women working there. Polly had said the building where the children lived was, essentially, the orphanage. They had a basic duty of care, but that was it, and it was mostly ignored.

They had been put here by people who didn't care and mostly forgotten about. It made her want to scream. Jennie knew those who worked at the mill didn't bother with the children, but it was too much.

"Why have you come up here?" she asked.

Maurice sighed and settled on the floor beside her. The moonlight came through the window and bathed their area in silvery light. Maurice leaned his back against the wall and made a face.

"Mother and Father are arguing again," he answered. "It's getting worse, and I wanted to get away from it."

"Do they argue a lot?"

"Only in the last couple of years. But it's bad lately. I don't know why it is, but Mother said it's something they had to sort out between themselves. It's a bit difficult to ignore it all when they're shouting loud enough that I can hear them in my room."

Jennie stared at him.

"I thought your family was happy enough."

"What made you think we're happy?" Maurice grunted. "Just because we're the ones living in the big, grand house supposedly looking down on all of you?"

"I didn't mean it like that…"

"I bet you did, though. Everyone else does."

"But I don't see you like that, though," Jennie protested. "I am envious of what you have, but I don't think that way."

Maurice frowned.

"Why are you envious?"

Jennie felt comfortable talking to Maurice. They didn't talk often as Mr Cooper didn't want his son to be friends with the children who worked so close to the house, but Maurice often snuck over to see them. The two of them had become friends, although Jennie did worry that she would be found out and get punished. Maurice had kept his word to not say anything, though, and she appreciated it.

One more person she could rely on. That became three people. It was hard to find people she could turn to when you were stuck in the middle of nowhere and most of the children were rude and unruly. No one wanted to be there, but the circumstances meant they had no choice.

From the look of it, Maurice was in the same position despite things being slightly better for him.

"So why are you here?" Maurice looked at her, pulling his legs up to rest his arms on his knees. "You look like you've been crying."

"I…" Jennie wanted to deny it and say she wasn't, but another tear fell, and she swiped at her face with her sleeve. "When your father met me two years ago, I was separated from my brother."

"Your little brother, right? I remember you telling me."

"He was four then. He would be six now." Jennie's chest squeezed as she remembered the last time she saw Stephen. "Mr

Cooper wasn't going to take him with us as he was too young, and I made him promise that he would bring Stephen here when he was old enough. He agreed."

Maurice frowned.

"It sounds like he had no intention of doing what you wanted. He has a habit of doing that."

"But he shook my hand!" Jennie protested. "A decent person shakes hands on a promise and keeps the promise. And he didn't."

"Maybe he thought you were going to forget, and he didn't have to worry about it."

That's what Jennie had guessed when she tried to talk to Mr Cooper earlier in the day. He had no intention of doing as she wanted. It was just to pacify her so she would do whatever he wanted, which was to behave. She rubbed her hands over her face.

"It was the only thing that was keeping me going over the years. I just wanted to see my brother again. I still remember the last time I saw him, when he was banging at the window crying for me as I went into the carriage to come here. I didn't get to say goodbye properly, they just…"

"And Father lied to you," Maurice said quietly.

"I thought he would be somewhat decent with that, but he wasn't. He's a horrible man, and now…I want to get away from here."

"What do you mean?"

"I mean I want to run away." Jennie scrambled to her feet and began to pace around the room, kicking the wall before walking back to Maurice, her hands waving in the air. "I wanted to stay with my brother. But I was given no choice. I made a promise to my parents to look after my brother, and I broke mine because of your father. I don't want to be here if I'm not going to get what I asked for. Wanting my brother to be with me isn't too much to ask, is it?"

"I don't have any siblings, so I wouldn't know the sentiment. But I take your point."

Jennie wiped at her face again. She was fed up with crying; it was making her head hurt.

"I want to go back to London," she declared. "I want to get away from here and back to London. I must find my brother."

"But how are you going to do that?" Maurice demanded. "You're a child! Nobody is going to help a little girl wandering around looking for her sibling. If anything, you'll end up in a worse situation than you were before."

Jennie snorted.

"I can take care of myself."

"Jennie, I'm ten years old, and I know that I would certainly not be able to take care of myself on my own. You're younger than me. How can you manage it?"

Jennie faltered. He had a point. How was she supposed to cope if Maurice was certain he couldn't? She wanted to say that things would be different, and she knew it would be fine, but her determination was fading.

She knew, right then, that she had lost her brother. And there was going to be very little chance of finding him again. Maybe none.

She burst into tears, unable to stop them.

"I don't want to lose him," she whispered. "He's all I've got left."

"I know." Maurice stood and approached her, patting her awkwardly on the shoulder. "I know."

That just seemed to make Jennie cry even harder.

CHAPTER 4

Jennie shivered and wrapped her thin coat around her as the wind whipped around her. It was so cold, and she could feel her teeth chattering. Being up on a hill, the wind seemed to be strong, and it would threaten to knock everyone over. Jennie was surprised nothing had fallen off the roof.

She stood on the driveway and stared out across the fields ahead. She could just about see the main road in the distance. It looked close enough that she could walk it, and then all she had to do was follow it. Given none of the adults cared about her, she might be missed but nobody would come looking for her. If she got far enough away, they would forget about her.

Could she just try…

"What are you doing out here?"

Jennie gasped and spun around. Mrs Cooper had come out of the house, bundled up in her thick coat, frowning at her in surprise. Jennie licked her chapped lips.

"I…I…"

"Why aren't you at work?" Mrs Cooper looked her up and down. "You should go inside, girl. You're shaking."

Jennie wanted to say that it wasn't much warmer inside, but she kept her mouth closed. While Mrs Cooper was a little nicer than her husband, she wasn't much better. Also, the woman might figure out what she was planning.

Even though Maurice said she wouldn't be able to get back to London on her own, Jennie found herself determined to prove him wrong. She wanted to try.

It wasn't going to happen right now, though. The winter had set in only a few days ago, and it was bad. There were murmurs of snow on the horizon, and Jennie didn't want to escape now and get caught in the snow. That was a recipe for disaster. She had to bide her time.

Even if the longer she was away from Stephen made it more painful.

"Did you hear me?" Mrs Cooper prompted. "Go inside and warm up. I'm sure the fires are burning by now."

Jennie bowed her head and hurried away. The reality was, there was one fire, but it was in the dining room, and there were too many children to huddle around to get warm. It was like the adults didn't care if so many of their children got sick due to the cold and lack of food, seeing as their meals had become rather limited.

She was surprised that anyone was able to work in those conditions. She was sure she could feel her ribs clearly through her skin.

Maybe it was a good thing Stephen wasn't here. He would have suffered more than anyone else. But that didn't stop Jennie from wanting to leave.

Heading into the building, Jennie went into the dining room. The tables had been pushed away from the fireplace, and many of the children were up as close to it as they could without getting their clothes caught on fire. The ones towards the back were still shivering, indicating that the heat was either not that good or was being blocked by the other bodies.

William and Polly were at the back, William sitting on the table while Polly rubbing his arms. He was shivering more than Jennie; his face so pale she was surprised that he was upright. Jennie joined them.

"Is he all right?" she asked.

"He's burning up," Polly said grimly.

"But it's so...cold..." William said through chattering teeth. "I'm so...c-cold..."

"You have a fever, William. We need to get you by the fire and get you warm."

Jennie touched her fingers to her friend's cheek, shocked by how warm he was. They were nowhere near the fire, but he might as well be sitting in the flames.

"Isn't there anything we can do?" She looked pleadingly at Polly. "He's sick."

"We just took him to the infirmary." Polly scowled. "Matron told us that he looked fine, and he wasn't that bad, so we had to come back."

"I...I can't...work like this," William whimpered. "My...my fingers..."

He held out his hands, and Jennie saw his fingers were curled, looking frozen in place. Jennie was sure his skin was turning blue at the fingertips. She wanted to cry at the sight of her friend practically freezing in front of her.

"He's clearly not well," she protested. "How can they say he's not that bad?"

"The infirmary is full. Matron has no extra beds, and she is overrun."

"That's not an excuse!"

Polly pressed her lips together, showing her unhappiness.

"I understand your frustration, but it's not going to make anyone do anything, is it?" she snapped. "We're not important enough to be heard."

"Even though William could get worse if he's not looked after?"

Polly huffed and glared at her.

"Do you think you can do any better? Because I'd like to see you try. And I know you're terrified of Matron like everyone else."

She wasn't wrong about that. Jennie was terrified of the woman in charge of the infirmary. She reminded her of a dragon from one of the books she had been reading with Mr Lewis. A lot of fire came out of her, and Jennie didn't like going to her to say she had injured herself. The woman didn't have a maternal bone in her body.

"Let's get William to bed," Polly said, urging William off the table. "He might as well try and get some sleep before he's disturbed."

"What is Mrs Dobson going to say?" Jennie asked, helping William on his other side as they went towards the door.

Polly snorted, and that was answer enough for her. Jennie decided to leave it as it was because she could tell that her friend was close to losing her temper. Polly was very protective over both her and William, and to have him this sick and nobody would help was making her more agitated.

They were almost at the top of the stairs when Mrs Dobson came down them. She slowed in surprise when she saw them.

"What are you doing?"

"We're taking William to get some sleep, Mrs Dobson," Polly replied.

"But you're not supposed to be in the bedrooms during the day. You know that."

"He's sick! He needs to rest."

"Then take him to the infirmary."

Polly growled, and Jennie could tell she was close to snapping at the woman. She spoke hurriedly.

"Matron is overwhelmed, and we didn't want to bother her. It won't be for long, Mrs Dobson."

Mrs Dobson didn't look happy about that. Then she sighed and nodded.

"All right. But don't take…"

She didn't get any further before William collapsed, taking Polly and Jennie with him. They caught him before he hit his head on the stairs, but he was such a heavy weight that Jennie almost dropped him again.

"William!" They turned him over and Jennie shook his shoulders. "William!"

But William was unconscious, practically limp on the floor.

JENNIE STOOD at the end of William's bed, watching as the matron attempted to pull the sheet over his head. But Polly got in the way and sagged to her knees beside the little boy, sobbing as she leaned over and hugged him.

"Please, William," she whispered. "Please wake up. Stop scaring us. Wake up!"

The matron looked like she was about to cry as well. Jennie was surprised at that; the woman was normally so cold and strict that it made a trip to the infirmary scary for her, but now she saw that Matron had tears in her eyes. She laid a hand on Polly's shoulder.

"I'm sorry, Polly," she said, her Scottish accent thicker than normal. "He's gone. You need to step back."

"No!" Polly wailed. "He's not dead! He can't be!"

A sigh from Mrs Dobson made Jennie jump. She had completely forgotten that the nasty lady was there as well. Then she appeared behind Matron and urged her aside to take Polly by the arms.

"Come along, dear," she said gently, urging Polly to her feet as the girl sobbed. "We have to do this."

Polly was still crying as she was led to another bed, where Mrs Dobson made her sit down. Matron glanced at Jennie, lowering the sheet for a moment.

"Do you need a moment?" she asked.

Jennie was not used to any of this kindness. They were being gentle with her and Polly, and it was strange. She was half-expecting them to turn back to their usual state of being unkindness, as if they were hoping to lower their guard. It made Jennie feel very uncomfortable.

She moved around to the side of the bed and looked down at William. He looked so peaceful, as if he was sleeping. If he had no colour in his cheeks, she might have believed it. He had taken his last breath only a few moments before, with nobody able to do anything to save him. His sickness was too far gone.

Jennie reached out and touched his hand. It was stiff and ice-cold. It made her shiver, and her throat closed. William had been sickly for the whole time she had known him, but to see him dead was shocking. She never thought it would happen to him, and yet here he was. It felt like a bad dream.

She leaned over and kissed his forehead.

"Safe journeys, William," she whispered. "Hopefully, you'll be looked after better where you're going."

She didn't look at Matron to see if she heard it, stepping back and watching as the woman put the sheet over William's face. Polly's sobs got louder, and she buried her face in her hands. Mrs Dobson had left her to cry, walking away so speak to Matron. Jennie went to her friend and sat beside her. Immediately, the two of them embraced, and Jennie had to squeeze her eyes tightly shut as Polly cried onto her shoulder.

"I can't believe he's gone," she whimpered. "I knew he was sick, but I never thought…"

"I know." Jennie felt tears trickling down her cheeks, making them sting. "I know."

She found herself thinking back to her parents dying. She had been shocked and scared at the time, realizing someone that she loved was gone, and she was becoming more and more alone. After that, and losing her brother, Jennie had vowed never to get close to someone like that again. But she had gotten close to William, a sweet little boy who was good company.

He loved life, even when stuck in the factory and terrible conditions. And he wasn't here anymore.

The pain of losing someone was still bad. And Jennie hated it.

"Why do we have to die for anyone to take notice?" Polly lifted her head and wiped at her face. "I can't believe this is happening to us. Why did it have to be William?"

"I don't know." Jennie pressed the heels of her hands into her eyes, hoping they would stop the tears. "He didn't deserve this."

"None of us do. But they don't care about us." Polly's voice had taken on a bitter tone. "They're planning to work us until we can't anymore and then force us to work even more. It's just horrible."

Jennie couldn't agree more with that. Even though they were currently getting sympathy from a few of the people who worked there, it wouldn't last for long. It was not something she could get used to. Neither did she want to get used to knowing that the only way to get out of a job was to die.

She couldn't stay here any longer.

"We have to get out of here," she whispered.

Polly stared at her.

"But…how are we going to do that? They're never going to let us leave."

"We'll think of something. We must get away from here. Escape to something better."

"Like what?"

Jennie snorted and gestured at their surroundings.

"Anything is better than what we've got here. We are being worked to exhaustion, and that can't happen. We need to leave sooner rather than later."

Polly looked as if she wasn't convinced. Jennie could see why: they were children. She was eight, and Polly was barely ten. How would they be able to cope if they were able to escape from here? They could be resourceful, but if they did it during the winter, would they survive? Even if they waited until it was warmer, there was no guarantee they would have a better life.

Jennie was adamant about it, though. She believed they would have better no matter what they were doing, if they weren't in the factory and the workhouse. This would be what their life would be, and the thought left her terrified.

She was not going to remain here.

"Jennie? Polly?"

Jennie looked around. Maurice was approaching them. From his flushed face and untidy appearance, he looked like he had come over in a rush. She almost burst into tears seeing him.

"I heard about William. I thought..." He looked over at the bed, and his face paled. "Oh, no."

Jennie couldn't say anything. She simply nodded. Polly stared at him.

"Your father isn't going to be happy that you're in here," she pointed out.

"I don't care about that," Maurice declared. "He can't stop me."

Polly gave him a watery smile. Then she jumped up and flung her arms around his neck. Maurice looked surprised that she was doing that, but then he started hugging her in response. Jennie watched them, her chest tightening at the sight. Polly was taking it the worst out of the three of them, and the sight of her coming apart when she was the one to look after everyone was shocking. She didn't like this side. She wanted things to go back to normal.

She wanted William back.

"Maurice!" Mr Cooper came hurrying into the infirmary, looking shocked that he was embracing someone. "What are you doing in here?"

"I was seeing my friends, Pa." Maurice didn't let go of Polly as he turned to his father. "William's dead."

Mr Cooper slowed, looking momentarily perplexed. Then he recovered and scowled in disapproval.

"That doesn't mean you should be coming in here and interacting with these children. You're better than that."

"Better than what?" Maurice challenged. "Better than people smaller than me dying because nobody's truly taking care of them? You said that you always looked after your charges, but it's very clear that you're not, Pa."

His father's eyes flashed, and Jennie thought he was going to strike his son. She gripped onto the edge of the bed, bracing herself for the fight that was incoming. Mr Cooper moved towards Maurice, who pushed Polly behind him.

"You do not get to talk to me like that, Maurice," he said in a low voice. "You're starting to get ideas above your place."

"My friend is dead, Pa! You think I shouldn't be able to comfort those who cared?"

"Enough." Mr Cooper grabbed his son by the arm and pulled him away. "You're coming with me. Now."

"Maurice!"

Polly tried to go after them, but Mr Cooper gave her such a glare that she shrank back. She sank onto the bed beside Jennie with a slight whimper. Mr Cooper gave the body under the sheet a cursory glare before turning it onto the girls.

"Get back to your tasks," he said sharply. "You've spent too much time in here. I'll make sure Mrs Dobson keeps you busy."

Then he was gone, dragging a protesting Maurice behind him. Polly bowed her head and began to sob, her body trembling. Her chest tight and unable to speak with her throat closing, Jennie put her arms around her friend's shoulders and held her close. She couldn't say anything to what had just happened.

But she could think about it. And the thoughts directed at Mr Cooper were making her even angrier than she thought possible.

CHAPTER 5

1859

"What do you think you're doing?"

Jennie's heart stopped when she heard Mr Cooper' voice. She looked up and saw him standing over her, his arms folded with a dark scowl on his face. For a moment, Jennie was unable to say anything. She was petrified, unable to believe that she had been caught. Nobody was supposed to know she was here, and yet Mr Cooper had found her.

"I…"

"You're supposed to be in bed," Mr Cooper snapped. "I saw a light from the window and thought we had an intruder. What are you doing?"

"I was…"

Then he caught sight of the book she was trying to hide behind her. Before Jennie could react, he reached down and snatched it out of her hands. Jennie tried to hold on, but she was pushed back against the wall. The rough bricks scraped against her back, and she couldn't help but cry out. Straightening up, Mr Cooper looked at the title on the spine.

"*Frankenstein* by Mary Shelley." His lip curled. "I can't believe you're reading something like this. Why are you reading when you're supposed to be working?"

"Because I want to read," Jennie managed to reply. She swallowed and pushed herself up to her feet. She was little compared to her employer, but she wasn't about to be cowed. "I enjoy it."

"You're not supposed to be reading! You have your lessons with Mr Lewis, and you're supposed to do your schoolwork with everyone else. You're not meant to be sneaking off to read books you shouldn't be reading at all!"

"What's wrong with *Frankenstein?*" Jennie demanded. "It's an interesting book."

Mr Cooper scoffed at that, turning it over in his hands.

"This is brand new. You haven't left the factory since you got here, so how did you get a book like this?"

That was when Jennie faltered. This would mean getting someone she liked into trouble. They might be able to look after themselves, but Jennie didn't want any further discord to happen. She knew how bad it was, even at her young age. She drew herself up to her full height and lifted her chin defiantly, saying nothing. Mr Cooper arched an eyebrow.

"You're not going to tell me how you got this book?"

Again, Jennie said nothing. She just stared at him. Mr Cooper shook his head and grabbed her arm.

"Come with me," he said, kicking over the candle Jennie had placed by her. It went out, and they were plunged into darkness.

"Let me go!" Jennie tried to pull away, crying out when his fingers dug into her arm. "What are you doing?"

"You're going to come with me, and we'll inspect my library." Mr Cooper dragged her behind him as they made their way back to the buildings across the field. "I know that I have a copy of this in my home. If it's not there, then I know you've been stealing from my home. That's not something I'm going to tolerate."

Jennie panicked. She knew what that meant, and the punishments they were given were just terrifying. She couldn't handle that.

"I didn't steal anything!" she cried. "It was a present!"

"A present?" Mr Cooper snorted. "Why would someone want to give you a present?"

"It's my birthday today! It's a birthday present!"

He stopped and looked at her. Jennie couldn't see his face, but she could guess what it looked like. It left her feeling cold knowing what he was thinking.

"You got a birthday present from someone?" Mr Cooper sounded like he didn't believe it. "Who would care enough to give you a nice book?"

"I promise you, it's a present!" Jennie protested.

"I don't believe you. Even if it is your birthday, you aren't worthy enough of presents." He started walking again. "Come along. If you really have stolen from me, you'll be severely punished."

"Like you punished Maurice?" Jennie shot back. The words were out of her mouth before she could stop them, but she kept going. "You've sent him away to another school far away from here because you don't want him interacting with us. You punished him by taking him to another part of the country."

"Shut up."

"Maurice didn't want to go, though, did he?" Jennie was practically screaming at him. "How could you treat your own child like that? He was my friend!"

"Silence!"

The smack came out of nowhere, and Jennie felt pain exploding in her face, her teeth rattling. It knocked her off-balance, and she stumbled. She would have fallen over if Mr Cooper hadn't been holding her up. She started to cry as she was yanked along again.

"You really need to learn your place, you little runt! You don't get to talk back to people like that, and if you haven't learned that in the time you've been here, there's something wrong with you."

Jennie was still sobbing, her face in agony, as they reached the courtyard. It had felt like a long walk from the edge of the field she had been using as a place to hide and have time to herself to the workhouse and factory, and her legs were screaming at her as she was pulled along faster than she was comfortable with. In her mind, she was panicking about what was going to happen. She couldn't let Mr Cooper take away her present, and she couldn't be punished for doing something she enjoyed.

They were almost at the house Mr Cooper and his wife used when she heard Mr Lewis' voice behind them.

"What's going on? What's with the noise?"

Jennie started crying harder when she heard his voice. The schoolteacher felt like a guardian angel. He had always looked out for her. He wouldn't let this happen.

Mr Cooper growled and turned to the approaching man, who was shrugging into his jacket. He looked like he had been working and fell asleep at his desk.

"This is nothing to do with you, Mr Lewis," he snapped. "Go back to what you were doing."

"What are you doing with Jennie?" Mr Lewis frowned at him before looking at Jennie. "She's crying. And what happened to her face? She's bleeding."

Jennie then felt something dribble over her lips, and she instinctively licked her top lip. The taste of it told her that it was blood. Her nose was bleeding. Had Mr Cooper hit her that hard?

"She snuck out when she was supposed to be sleeping and she stole something from me," Mr Cooper growled.

Mr Lewis' eyes widened.

"What did she steal? Jennie's not the type to do that."

"You don't know her like I do, Lewis. She's a troublemaker."

"She's one of my best pupils, Cooper." Mr Lewis folded her

arms, his expression tensing. "You're accusing her of stealing that book in your hand, I'm guessing?"

"Of course! She snuck into my house and stole it from my library." Mr Cooper shook Jennie, making her cry out. "She's been pushing the boundaries too much lately. She's been unproductive lately, and now I know why."

"That book?" Mr Lewis looked confused, and then he took the book from Mr Cooper before the other man could stop him. "But this is the book I gave Jennie."

"What?"

"It's her birthday today, and she's an avid reader, so I thought she might like this." He opened it. "If you'd looked at the first page, you would have seen a birthday note from me. This is her book."

Mr Cooper looked like he had just been hit over the head. His grip loosened on Jennie's arm, and she took that as a chance to pull away and run to Mr Lewis. She cowered behind him, shaking so hard in the warm May night that her teeth were chattering.

"You got it for her?" Mr Cooper sounded stunned. "Why would you bother with a child like her? She's nothing."

"You might think that, but she's a bright girl. There's a lot of potential for her, and I wanted to bring it out."

"Even though she's neglecting her jobs by spending all night reading?"

"She does her work despite everything," Mr Lewis snapped back. "Just because she doesn't do as you want every second of the day doesn't mean she's a troublemaker."

Mr Cooper practically bared his teeth at him, but Mr Lewis didn't blink. Jennie's heart was racing so fast that she felt lightheaded.

"If you're going to punish Jennie for her love of reading, then you might as well punish all children who deserve to learn," Mr Lewis went on. "You shouldn't jump to conclusions, and if she's doing her work, then what is the problem? Unless you like to hurt children because you're not brave enough to stand up to men your own size?"

"Why, you..." Mr Cooper snarled, but Mr Lewis turned and pushed the book into Jennie's hands.

"Go back to bed, Jennie," he urged. "I'll deal with this. You need to get some sleep."

"Yes, Mr Lewis."

Jennie wasn't about to argue with him about that. Clutching her book to her chest, she ran for the workhouse. She didn't want to be around Mr Cooper any longer. Her eyes still stinging with tears, she ran inside and slumped to her knees on the stairs, waiting for her heart to stop racing.

How was she going to get out of this now?

* * *

"Jennie?"

Jennie looked around. Mr Lewis had entered the dining room and was standing just inside the door. He beckoned her to join him. Shoving the last of her breakfast into her mouth - she was so used to it that it didn't make her gag anymore - she stood up and gave Polly a smile across the table.

"I'll see you in the factory," she said.

Polly nodded, her expression worried.

"What have you done?" she whispered.

"I'll let you know."

This was probably about the standoff from the night before. Jennie had wondered how things had gone from that, but she had been too scared to find out. She was just relieved she wasn't punished for supposedly stealing a book from him. It was not how she wanted to spend her birthday.

Leaving the dining room with Mr Lewis, she followed the schoolteacher down the hall to the end. There was a window that looked down into the main courtyard, and Mr Lewis stopped there, staring out into the yard. Jennie joined him and saw Mr Cooper arguing with his wife. Neither of them looked particularly happy, but that was normal for them now.

Ever since Mr Cooper had sent Maurice off to boarding school on the other side of the country, his wife had been showing her obvious resentment. She wasn't very nice, either, but at least she had loved her son. They had been fighting ever since.

It had been more than six months, and Jennie still missed Maurice.

"How's your face?" Mr Lewis asked, glancing at her. "You have bruises on your face."

"I'll live." Jennie managed a tiny smile. "I'm used to it."

He frowned.

"Nobody should ever have to be used to that. Not even children."

"It's all I've known for the last three years, Mr Lewis."

He grimaced, and Jennie wanted to cry again. In all the time she had been here, the schoolteacher was the only person who showed her kindness and never expected anything in return. Mrs Dobson and Matron would on occasion, but then they would go back to being strict and nasty, and Jennie didn't like it.

"I'm sorry you had to go through all of that last night," he said suddenly. He leaned his hands on the windowsill, his head bowed. He looked more worn out than the children. "Mr Cooper shouldn't have been so cruel towards you."

"He doesn't believe that I didn't steal that book. And you gave it to me."

"I know. And he did manage to see that it wasn't one of his books, and you couldn't have stolen from him. But the fact he was adamant to believe it, and is still dubious about the fact I gave you a birthday present…"

"Why is he so awful?" Jennie asked. "I don't understand."

"He's just so full of hate. And I think being in charge here when he has the power doesn't help, either."

"Why are you here? Don't you hate working here?"

Mr Lewis didn't answer, and Jennie thought she might have been too forward. Then he turned and looked at her.

"I want to make sure the children have something in their lives that isn't working for other people when they should be growing up."

Jennie stared. She hadn't had a conversation like this with the schoolteacher, and it threw her a little. It took a moment for her to get her voice back.

"I…why don't you do something about it? Get us out of here?"

"If I had the money and resources, I absolutely would. But there's only so much I can do in the situation. So I must do what I'm able to. Which is to teach children and give them something that's not being stuck under a machine and…you know…" He shuddered. "I'm sure you remember the accident last month."

Jennie did. One of the boys had been crushed in between the machines when he wasn't fast enough. He had died quickly, and Jennie still saw the blood on the floor that hadn't been cleaned up properly. The boy was William's age, and he had let his attention wander.

Her stomach clenched thinking about William. She missed the little boy. He had been very sweet and knew how to make her smile. Even with their surroundings, he was an innocent child. He was one of the few who deserved to get out of there. In a way, he had, but not in the way he would have wanted.

At least he wouldn't be suffering now.

Jennie blinked away the tears and rubbed at her eyes. She was not going to cry.

"I don't want to be here anymore, Mr Lewis," she said. "I want to run away and do something else. Anything that isn't this."

"I know, Jennie. I understand, but you know that the world is tough out there, if not tougher than in here."

"Anything's better than being in here," Jennie muttered bitterly. "If I get attacked for reading on my birthday…"

"I know." Mr Lewis placed a hand on her shoulder. "You are still very young, but you're tougher than you think. You'll be able to leave here. I know you will."

"But how?"

He smiled and squeezed her shoulder before pulling back.

"You must be resourceful. You must be smart. And you must be two steps ahead of everyone else. If you can manage that, you'll be able to run rings around someone like Mr Cooper."

"Jennie!" Mrs Dobson appeared in the doorway, frowning as she beckoned her sharply. "Come along! You've got to get to work!"

Jennie gave Mr Lewis a small smile before hurrying away. She joined Polly as the children filed out of the dining room, the older girl clasping her hand.

"What did he want?" Polly asked.

"I'll tell you later," Jennie whispered back. She could see Mrs Dobson watching her, and she didn't want to get into trouble again. If Mr Cooper had mentioned something, then people would be watching her closer.

She just wanted to get through the day without another punishment.

CHAPTER 6

1864

"We have visitors!" Polly cried, stopping at the window to stare into the yard.

"What?" Jennie looked up, brushing her sweaty hair out of her eyes. "What did you say? My ears are ringing."

"We have visitors!" Polly beckoned her over. "Come and have a look!"

Wiping her hands on the cloth tucked into her belt, Jennie joined her friend and they both looked out. A carriage in dark brown with a coat of arms on the door had turned up in the courtyard. A tall, elegant-looking man wearing a black coat with fur on the collar, his hair iron-grey with a thick beard and moustache, was getting out. Mr Cooper was there, and the two men shook hands firmly. They looked like old friends.

Jennie wasn't even aware that Mr Cooper had any friends. He wasn't a very likeable person.

"I wonder who it is," she said. "What do you think he wants?"

"I overheard Mrs Dobson talking to Matron the other day," Polly said, turning to her. Her eyes were shining. "Apparently, there's going to be someone here to seek young workers to go with him."

"Young workers?" Jennie frowned. "He's looking for people like us to work for him?"

"That sounds about right."

"But why Mr Cooper? He needs us for the factory. Wouldn't he lose workers if he gives some of the young workers to someone else?"

Polly shrugged.

"I don't know about that. All I know is that we might have a chance of getting out of here! We could leave!"

Jennie had to admit that the thought had floated across her mind, but she didn't want to entertain it. After all, she had been promised by Mr Cooper that her brother could join them at the workhouse and factory when he was old enough, but that hadn't happened. She had given up hope of ever seeing him again.

And she has given up on believing she would leave unless it was in a wooden box. Maybe that would be too much to think the children would get a coffin of any sort and would just get unceremoniously tossed into a shallow grave. That had happened to William. Six years on, and Jennie still remembered the moment. It was too much for her and it had left her in a state of hysterics afterwards, knowing that only she and Polly had truly cared about William's welfare.

"There isn't much of a guarantee that we'll be chosen, though," she pointed out. "We might not get looked at as potential workers."

Polly pouted, tossing her hair over her shoulder.

"Honestly, Jennie, you need to be optimistic. This might be a chance for us to get out of here!"

"After all this time, I've lost faith in pretty much anything."

"But it would be nice to get away from this place, wouldn't it?

I know you've wanted it for a long time. Probably as soon as you got here." Polly took Jennie's hand. "It's been eight years for you, and almost ten for me. We deserve better."

She was right, but Jennie was still reluctant. She could recall the day she entered the orphanage in London and was separated from Stephen. She remembered making Mr Cooper promise with a handshake that he would bring Stephen with him when he was old enough so they could be together. That man had broken the promise, and Jennie had lost faith in anything working in her favour.

Sure, she did have luck in a strong friendship with Polly and a kind schoolteacher in Mr Lewis, but she was still unsure about having faith getting what she wanted.

It hadn't worked for the last eight years.

"Jennie! Polly!"

Mr Lewis was walking through the machines towards them. Polly tensed, and Jennie wondered if they were going to get into trouble for not doing their jobs. Then she remembered something: Mr Lewis stayed in the schoolroom or his study. He never came into the actual factory itself. So seeing him here was a surprise.

She approached him.

"Is something wrong?" she asked, using the cloth she tugged out of her belt to wipe her forehead. It was far too warm in there, and she needed a drink for her dry throat.

"Mr Cooper wants to see you two," Mr Lewis replied.

"What?" Polly joined Jennie; her voice barely audible over the sound of the machines. "What does he want?"

"I don't know. He just told me to come and find you. Like I'm one of his workers." Mr Lewis looked annoyed at that. "Anyway, you two come with me. He wants you quickly."

Jennie looked at Polly and saw the same thoughts on her friend's face. It was the height of summer, but it was so warm in the factory that stepping outside felt like a blessing. They weren't going to waste another second if they were being told they could leave.

Following the schoolteacher, they left the factory, and Jennie breathed a sigh of relief as she and Polly walked out into the sunshine. There was a gentle breeze, and it tickled her warm cheeks. That felt a lot better, and Jennie clasped Polly's hand in a grateful grip. Her friend leaned into her and, for some reason, the two of them started giggling. Mr Lewis gave them bemused looks, but Jennie didn't know how to explain it. Somehow, they just wanted to laugh.

She wondered if they were going to end up in the insane asylum with the way things were going. Her mind was certainly twisting things around until she felt like she was going mad.

If they were lucky - and she wasn't holding out hope on it - they might have different circumstances soon. They just had to behave themselves and hope that Mr Cooper didn't stop them from getting a better chance.

They entered his house, and Mr Lewis led them across the hallway and towards a closed door. He knocked twice, and then they heard Mr Cooper' voice.

"Come in!"

The schoolteacher turned to the two girls and nodded encouragingly at them.

"In you go." He gave them a smile. "It's going to be fine."

Jennie and Polly exchanged glances. Then the man opened the door, and they walked in. Mr Cooper was leaning an arm on the mantelpiece talking to his visitor in one of the leather chairs, his legs crossed. Both were drinking something, holding large glasses. Jennie didn't know what it was they were drinking, but she could smell something in the air that made her wrinkle her nose. Mr Cooper frowned at them, clearly not happy to see them.

"These are two of the older children we have here. You can see how they match up to your expectations, Mr Harrison."

* * *

Mr Harrison sat up and gave both girls a look up and down. Jennie didn't know why, but the tension in her body relaxed a little. Just one look at him, and she knew he was a strict individual, but there was nothing cruel about him. Not like there was with Mr Cooper. He was different, although how, she couldn't put her finger on.

It was strange.

"How many children have you got who are fourteen and older?" Mr Harrison asked, standing up in one flowing movement and sauntering over to the girls.

"We have at least nine girls and thirteen boys right now," Mr Cooper answered.

"I don't need that many, but at least I've got enough to pick from." Mr Harrison observed Polly first. "What's your name?"

"Polly."

"How old are you?"

"Sixteen."

She drew herself a little taller, fixing Mr Harrison with a stare that made Jennie feel proud of her. Polly was a strong girl, someone who wasn't afraid to stand up for herself. It drove Mrs Dobson mad when they started talking back, but Polly had a lot of emotional strength behind her with her quick wit. It made Jennie want to be like her.

"How are you with food?" Mr Harrison questioned suddenly. "Have you baked bread before?"

"No, sir. I've always been in the factory."

"Would you like to try working in the kitchens instead?"

Polly blinked, looking stunned. Her mouth opened and closed as she tried to get her words again. Jennie wondered where this was going. Then she realized Mr Harrison was looking at her, his light blue eyes intense.

"And what about you?"

"I'm Jennie. I'm fourteen."

"Jennie?" Mr Harrison glanced back at Mr Cooper with an arched eyebrow. "Isn't this the one you were talking to me about before? The one you caught sneaking out from her bed in the middle of the night?"

"Some years ago, but that's her." Mr Cooper scowled at Jennie, his eyes glittering. "She hasn't done it since, though. She learned her lesson."

Jennie bit her lip to stop herself from smiling, and she heard Polly fight back a giggle. Both knew that Jennie had never stopped sneaking out. She went to a quiet place around the factory to read. Sometimes she went to Mr Lewis' quarters, where he would give her extra lessons and give her more books to read. It did mean she was a bit more tired than everyone else but knowing that she was getting what she enjoyed doing was enough for Jennie to feel better about it.

She wasn't about to tell Mr Cooper that, though. That would get both her and the school teacher into trouble, and she wasn't about to do that and cut off the only time she could stay sane.

"What would you say about their work ethic?" Mr Harrison walked behind the girls and stopped. Jennie wanted to turn and look at him, but she forced herself to stay still, even if the hairs on the back of her neck prickled. "Are they hard workers?"

"They are probably the hardest workers out of the children I have here. They keep their heads down, for the most part, and do what they're told. Mrs Dobson does report they have moments where they're talking back and they do get punished for it, but when it comes to their work these two are the first ones to finish without complaint."

"I see." Mr Harrison paused. "And what about their literacy and numeracy? They need to know the basics for what I've got planned."

Mr Cooper straightened up. Did he suddenly look pleased?

"Polly and Jennie are always the same in their lessons. Both are good with numbers, and I know Jennie can read well."

From the way he said that Jennie knew he remembered the incident where he caught her reading on her ninth birthday. It had been some years back, but it was still fresh how she had been accused of theft when she hadn't done anything.

It was still a sore point for her.

"That's going to be an advantage for these two." Mr Harrison walked around them away, sipping from his glass before addressing Jennie and Polly. "I'm looking for some children to work in my flour mill. Some will be in the mill itself, and the rest will be in the bakery we have attached to it. We supply bread to most of the town we live in."

"Where do you live?" Polly asked.

"It's a village called Houghton in Cambridgeshire. It's a few hours north of here. Very quiet, out in the middle of nowhere, but we get a lot of business."

"And if you wanted us to work for you, would we be working in the mill?"

He looked amused that she was talking, and Jennie was halfway to saying to her friend maybe they should keep quiet. But Mr Harrison spoke candidly.

"Some of you will. Others will be working in the bakery, where you will make the bread or whatever we've been asked to make. You will be shown what to do by the workers already there if I think you'll be better fitted for that."

"And what about lessons?" Jennie questioned. "Will we still have our school lessons?"

The amused expression turned to her, and Jennie had to force herself to remain where she was when she wanted to shuffle backwards. Mr Harrison looked her up and down.

"You're at an age where you don't need to worry about your lessons anymore," he replied. "You're going to be working for all hours of the day. There won't be any time for lessons."

Jennie's heart sank. She really didn't want to stop those. They made her feel like she was doing something good with her life, and to have that taken away…

"I can see you're not too happy about that," Mr Harrison remarked. "I would've thought children would do anything to not do any school lessons at all."

"But I enjoy it," Jennie protested. "It's something different, and I love to read."

"Oh, really?"

Jennie knew she was talking too much, and she closed her mouth, biting her lower lip to stop herself. His look curious, Mr Harrison regarded her with a tilt of his head.

"What do you want to do with your life?" he asked her. "Do you have any aspirations?"

"I want to be a schoolteacher."

Mr Cooper scoffed at that, but Mr Harrison ignored him.

"Really?"

"I love to learn, sir," Jennie said eagerly. "I feel happy when I'm reading, and I help with the smaller children when they need help. Mr Lewis allows me to be his assistant most days."

Then she realised she was saying too much and stopped talking, glancing at Polly, who gave her a warning look. There was only so much they should talk about with the adults around them, otherwise they got into trouble for saying too much. Mr Harrison looked at Mr Cooper.

"Is this true?"

"I don't know," Mr Cooper replied in a blase manner. "I believe Mr Lewis has a bit of a soft spot for her, but I don't pay attention as long as they're doing their jobs."

"I see." Mr Harrison turned back to Jennie. "At your age, you would be expected to work and not carry on your education, but if you're adamant about it, I can make arrangements for you to continue."

Jennie felt her spirits lift.

"Pardon me? Really?"

"But you must show to me that you're not doing it to get out of working. You still must work for me. I'm not about to have anyone not do what they're told."

Jennie nodded quickly.

"Of course, Mr Harrison. I know that. And I can do whatever you need."

Mr Harrison looked mildly impressed. Jennie watched as he sipped his drink before moving away, nodding at Mr Cooper.

"She's precocious, isn't she? There's a wisdom about her that I didn't expect."

Mr Cooper snorted.

"I wouldn't call her wise, sir. Jennie's a hard worker but I wouldn't trust what she says."

"How about you let me be the judge of that?" Mr Harrison gestured at Jennie and Polly. "I'll take these two with me. I'll see if you have any other children who can do what I want, but these two girls are coming with me."

Mr Cooper straightened up.

"At the usual price?"

"Of course. I wouldn't break a business deal like that."

That made the factory manager smirk. He jerked his head towards the door when he gave Jennie and Polly a glare.

"Be off with you. You'll be leaving first thing in the morning."

The girls weren't about to respond to that. They practically scurried out of the room. It wasn't until they were outside that they began to squeal, hugging each other as they jumped around.

"I can't believe it!" Polly cried. "We're actually going to be leaving here!"

"I know! Someone was looking down on us today." Jennie felt her smile hurting her cheeks. "It'll be the last time we have to be in a factory."

"Although we are going to a mill. I'm sure it's going to be just as noisy."

"But it's a new place. We'll be away from here. And Mr Harrison seems like a decent man." Jennie looked towards the closed door. "Although I wonder why he came all the way down here when he lives several hours away."

"Do we need to think about that? We're going somewhere new!" Polly danced away, singing to herself. "I can't believe it's happening. We'll be gone, and we don't have to see this place again."

Jennie followed her, feeling the happiness well up in her chest. For eight years, she had been praying to leave and go somewhere else. Now it felt like her prayers were finally being answered.

They would be gone, and she could finally breathe.

CHAPTER 7

It took a whole day to get to the mill in Cambridgeshire, with the carriage setting off at dawn. The excitement at knowing they would be leaving was enough to keep Jennie and Polly awake most of the night. They could hardly settle down, knowing they would be leaving. Jennie was worried that if she fell asleep, she would wake up and find it was a dream to scare her into thinking she was hallucinating.

But when she went outside and saw Mr Harrison's carriage waiting for them, their meagre belongings being put inside, Jennie knew it wasn't a dream. They were going.

The only sad part was leaving Mr Lewis. He had been so kind to her over the years, and Jennie started to cry knowing that she might never see him again. But he hugged her, assured her how proud he was, and then gifted her at least a dozen books as a farewell present. Mr Harrison had been rather surprised that he would do that, but he didn't say anything when the books were put into the carriage as well.

It didn't take long to get to a train station, which Mr Harrison said would take them into London, where they would change trains to head into the Cambridgeshire countryside. From there they would travel a short journey by carriage to the mill.

Jennie had never been on a train before, and she felt like a little girl again when she saw the engine and three carriages attached to it at the station. The fumes made her eyes water, but that didn't stop her excitement. Polly was the same, practically stuck to the window as she looked out, watching the world go by.

The journey was long, and it was very busy when they got to London. Jennie and Polly stuck close to Mr Harrison, who managed to get a compartment for them alone. They ate once they were there, Mr Harrison treating them to simple meals that were the most delicious things the girls had eaten in a long time.

Jennie's stomach hurt after eating so much, aware that the food wasn't going to be the same when they got to the mill, and she wanted to make the most of it.

Their new employer was quite affable despite his appearance. He asked them questions about their lives, about their friendship and their education. When he looked through the books Mr Lewis had given Jennie, he was surprised by the content. Jennie felt a little embarrassed, but she was adamant about keeping them. This was the first time in years she had owned something that belonged solely to her.

She would make sure of it.

The sun was setting by the time they reached the station in Huntingdon, the town nearest to Houghton, and then they took a carriage to the mill. Polly had been flagging over the day as tiredness caught up with her, and she fell asleep as soon as she entered the carriage. Jennie had to stop herself from giggling as her friend snored, her head on Jennie's shoulder.

"You're going to have to wake your friend soon," Mr Harrison said, giving Polly an amused look. "You'll be sleeping in beds once you get there. I want you fresh and ready for the morning."

"We'll do our best, Mr Harrison," Jennie replied. "We just need some sleep, and we'll be ready."

"You do understand that things are going to be different with me than with Mr Cooper, don't you?"

"Of course. We're ready to work hard and do whatever is needed."

Jennie knew that things would likely not be any different from what she had been used to, but the scenery was different, the work would be something else, and she didn't have to worry about Mr Cooper turning up suddenly to make their lives more difficult. Ever since he caught her reading, he had tried to do it since, and Jennie had managed to be a little sneakier with it. It would be nice not to do that anymore.

"Were you telling me the truth, Jennie?" Mr Harrison asked suddenly.

"What about?"

"About wanting to become a teacher. You weren't telling me lies, were you?"

Jennie frowned.

"Why would I tell a lie about that, sir? I'm not one of those people who would do that. We get into serious trouble for lying, and I don't have the strength to keep it up."

Mr Harrison sat back and watched her in silence for a moment. Jennie wanted to squirm, but she stopped herself. And she couldn't, anyway, with Polly leaning on her shoulder as she slept. Finally, the mill owner spoke.

"You are a very candid person," he said finally. "That's not a quality you see in someone so young."

"You must grow up fast in a workhouse, Mr Harrison. And while I know my place, I don't want to be afraid to speak my mind."

"As long as you do know your place and understand where the boundaries are, you will go far in life."

Jennie didn't know how to answer that. She looked out of the window, seeing the sun setting behind the trees, casting a dark orange and golden glow across the leaves and the grass. It looked beautiful. There was something refreshing about being somewhere else that wasn't the middle of a desolate landscape in Surrey.

Things might not change, but Jennie had some hope for it.

Houghton was a tiny village, and it looked like it was dead as the carriage passed through, nobody out in the streets. Jennie craned her head to look, wondering if she would see anyone, but there was nothing.

"Houghton is a very quiet place," Mr Harrison said, as if sensing what she was thinking. "There is a lot of business at the mill, but it's mostly a sleepy village."

"Do they not mind the noise?"

"Not that I know of. Most of the people living here work at the mill, anyway, so they can hardly complain."

Jennie didn't know how to respond to that. It just looked like a larger version of the workhouse, just a lot nicer. But it couldn't be any worse, could it?

She hoped not. Otherwise, she and Polly had made a huge mistake being so excited.

THE FLOUR MILL was situated by the river, along with a row of cottages that looked out over the water. Mr Harrison had told Jennie that this would be where her and Polly would be staying, and they would have a shift pattern to adhere to. That would be dealt with in the morning after they had gotten some sleep. Jennie was glad they would get some rest before doing anything; she was exhausted.

Even doing nothing, her body felt like she had been doing a full day of work.

Polly woke up as the carriage stopped, rubbing her eyes as she climbed out and grabbed her bag. She looked up at the mill.

"It's huge," she breathed.

"It's a very productive place. You're going to need a big place when you're productive as you want more money coming in." Mr Harrison looked around and spied someone walking towards them with a look of surprise. "Byron? What are you doing here? I thought you were in Cambridge."

"I came back for the weekend, Father. I thought I'd surprise you."

Jennie couldn't stop herself from staring at the young man who joined them. He had to be at least sixteen years old, taller than both her and Polly with dark curly hair that was ruffled on his head. He was broad-shouldered and well-built, indicating that he had done a lot of labour himself.

Despite his youth, there were clear indications that he was Mr Harrison's son; his facial features were the same, as were the blue eyes. But there was an innocent glint in them that softened his features.

Jennie's heart stumbled over itself, and she closed her mouth when she realised her jaw had dropped.

"You certainly did." Mr Harrison smiled as he clapped a hand on the boy's shoulder. "Are you going to be helping out or have you got some studying to do?"

"That's all done. I thought I'd make myself useful, though."

"You don't need to, but I'm glad you are." Mr Harrison turned to the girls, both of whom were staring at the boy. "Forgive me, my son goes to school in Cambridge and spends his holidays with us."

Byron grinned at them, and Jennie was surprised to hear Polly giggling. She looked at her friend and saw her cheeks turning bright pink. Mr Harrison coughed and nudged his son into moving.

"Why don't you show Polly and Jennie to where they're going to be living? Emma and Mary can look after them after that. I've got to go and check on the mill."

"Yes, Father." Byron picked up the bags. "Mother said that dinner will be ready soon. Mrs May is making roast pheasant."

"Don't make my stomach growl, Byron. I don't need that while I'm walking around checking everything." Mr Harrison nodded at Jennie and Polly. "Emma and Mary will look after you two. They will show you what to do and who to report to. Remember, keep your heads down."

"Yes, sir," both girls chimed.

Giving them a final look, Mr Harrison walked away. Byron beckoned them to follow him.

"Come on. It's getting late. If you're quick, you should be able to get some dinner."

"I hope so," Polly said as she fell into step beside him. "I'm starving!"

Jennie couldn't help but smile as her friend started walking with Byron. It was not a surprise that Polly found Byron attractive; she thought the same thing. She trailed after them, taking in their surroundings. There was something surprisingly tranquil about being here. It was certainly not Surrey.

The conditions were likely going to be just as bad as they were in the workhouse, but already Jennie was feeling optimistic. There was a chance of having something better, even while working for minimal pay. Jennie could see herself liking life here rather than under the thumb of Mr Cooper.

She just had to take a deep breath and remember not to draw too much attention to herself.

CHAPTER 8

*1**866*
"Jennie!"

Wiping the sweat off her forehead, aware that she was smudging flour all over her face, Jennie saw her new friend Emma waving at her, beckoning her over. Relieved to have a moment from moving heavy bags of flour, Jennie dusted her hands down her skirt and made her way out of the barn.

The small, wiry fifteen-year-old girl was waiting for her with a very tall man with white hair and spectacles. He was so tall that he was practically blocking out the sun. Emma looked tiny next to him, but she was small for her age so even Jennie towered over her.

The man gave her a stern look that made Jennie want to run the other way. But she wasn't going to let this stranger intimidate her.

"Jennie, this is Mr Davies," Emma said, not seeming to notice how she was dwarfed by the man. "He's the new schoolteacher for us."

"Schoolteacher?" Jennie frowned. "What happened to Miss Horne?"

"She had to go home and look after her sick parents in Manchester. It was very sudden." Emma bit her lip. "She said that she would come back soon, but I don't know if we'll see her again."

Jennie wished that she didn't talk like that. It wasn't the first time someone had left and didn't return. In the two years since she had come to Houghton, she had become acquainted with plenty of people, only to have many of them move on to different pastures. Sometimes it was for familial reasons, other times it was to get married. Jennie hoped that would happen for her one day.

But she had come to accept that she was likely going to end up remaining at the flour mill for the rest of her life. At sixteen, she was going to struggle to do anything beyond her current job. Nobody was going to take on someone her age, she was sure of that.

"I had a letter from a Mr Lewis," Mr Davies said, his voice low and deep as he looked down at Jennie from his great height. "You're acquainted with him, I take it?"

Jennie straightened up. She hadn't heard about her kindly teacher in a long time. She had wondered if she ever would. It was strange not seeing him every day.

"I know him. He taught me when I lived at the workhouse in Surrey."

Mr Davies looked at Emma and jerked his head. The lively little girl seemed to realise what he meant and scurried away after giving Jennie a curious look. She hurried off, and the man beckoned for Jennie to follow him. She was wary and wanted to remain where they were, but curiosity had gotten the better of her. This man knew Mr Lewis, and she had to know why.

She caught up with him as he reached the river, hurrying alongside him as he made huge, calculating strides. She had to crane her head back to look up at him.

"How do you know Mr Lewis?" she asked.

"We went to university together. I hadn't heard from him in years."

"Really?"

"I don't know how he found out, but he became aware that I was taking up a position here. He wrote to me and asked for me to look out for you." He seemed to scoff at that. "Make sure you continued your lessons and all that. I thought he was mad for asking me to help some child beyond their regular education, if I'm honest. It's not something I normally do."

Jennie bristled a little at his remark.

"You don't think that children who haven't got the money for the posh, fancy schools should have an education beyond the age of ten or something?"

"It's not up to me. I'm merely the teacher who does what he's told."

"Which is enough of an answer for me," Jennie shot back. "You don't think we should have a love of reading or writing, or anything involving learning. We're to simply work and keep our mouths closed."

Mr Davies blinked at her.

"I didn't say anything of the sort."

"You were pretty much implying it, Mr Davies. All children deserve to have the ability to learn and go on to greater things. If they show an affinity for something, shouldn't they show the passion for it? It's not how a teacher should behave. Mr Lewis understood that, and he was always kind towards us. He certainly encouraged me when he realised that I loved to read. I still have the books he gave me when I left, I treasure them every day."

Mr Davies was still staring at her. She knew that she was speaking very much out of turn, but Jennie hadn't been able to stop herself. Absently wiping her sweaty palms on her skirts, she stared at the water nearby, the sunlight glistening off the surface.

"I didn't mean to speak out of turn, sir," she mumbled. "My apologies."

"Mr Lewis did say that you were an intelligent girl beyond your years. Mr Harrison called you precocious. I can see what they mean."

Jennie didn't respond to that. She didn't know what to say. Finally, Mr Davies spoke again with a heavy sigh.

"I wasn't planning on following Mr Lewis' recommendation as I thought it was going to take you away from what was more important. But I can see why you're regarded quite highly. Even for a child of your age, people have good things to say about you, which I was not expecting at all."

That did make Jennie look up.

"What do you mean? Mr Harrison speaks highly of me?"

"Not just him. I was told by his son, Master Byron, that you're a tough, hardworking young lady who is incredibly bright and not given the chance to show it as you should." Mr Davies paused. "He also said that you're wasted here in the flour mill."

Jennie sighed.

"I think I am as well. But I can't exactly leave. I've got no family...that I know of."

She thought of Stephen but cast that thought aside. Her brother was either dead, still in the orphanage, or adopted into a family. She had no way of knowing anymore. It had been too long. Ten years and she had no idea if she was truly alone or not.

"Well, I wanted to see you for myself. It's not a usual thing for another colleague to recommend a child, especially for extra lessons. And it would get in the way of your work here."

"I can do both," Jennie insisted. "I managed at the age of eight to do both with extra lessons. I can handle it now."

"Are you certain about that?"

She nodded. Mr Davies arched an eyebrow and looked her up and down. It felt like she was being closely scrutinised, but she didn't back down. She had been given an opportunity to continue her education, and somehow Mr Harrison had agreed to it. She wasn't going to let it get away from her.

If it got her a chance to leave here and venture further out into something else, she would be taking it. Education was pretty much the only way to leave the mill. Jennie would do whatever she could to do that.

And to find her brother again. That was at the forefront of her mind.

"Fine." Mr Davies cleared his throat and turned away. "I'll see you in the schoolroom at seven-thirty, after your evening meal. We'll get started then."

"Yes, sir." Jennie gulped. "Thank you."

The new schoolteacher grunted, but he didn't look around. Jennie hurried back to the mill and found that she couldn't stop herself from smiling.

* * *

"Hiding away from working, are you?"

Jennie gasped and slammed her book shut, catching her finger between the pages. Her finger throbbing, she scrambled to her feet and put the book behind her back. Byron Harrison, Mr Harrison's son, was leaning against the tree trunk with his arms folded. He gave her a grin that made Jennie's heart skip.

"I…I mean…" She brushed her hair out of her eyes and tried not to be so flustered. "I don't know what you mean. I wasn't reading."

"Were you not?" Byron looked amused. "So you were just missing work to watch the sunset?"

Jennie felt her cheeks getting warm, and she looked at the ground. She knew Mr Davies and Mr Harrison had arranged for her to continue her education, but she had promised not to neglect her work. Now she was sneaking away to read when she was supposed to be making up the hours in the mill.

"You're not going to tell anyone about this, are you?" she whispered.

"Surely, someone's noticed that you've run away?"

"Polly and Emma have been covering for me," Jennie mumbled.

Byron didn't look surprised at that. Jennie wished he would stop staring. He was cute, and plenty of the girls who worked at the mill swooned over the owner's son. Jennie didn't want to be one of them, but she couldn't help herself.

"I suspected as much," Byron remarked. "They've always been looking out for you, ever since you came here."

Jennie blinked.

"You know about that?"

"I may not be around as much as my father, but I notice these things. And I'm aware of how hard working you are with everything going on around you." He held out a hand. "May I see what you're reading?"

Jennie hesitated. Should she be doing this? But she couldn't deny him when he asked. Bringing the book out, she held it out to him. Byron looked at the title.

"*Jane Eyre* by Charlotte Bronte. You like something like this, do you?"

"I prefer something a bit darker, but it's what I could get a hold of from Mr Davies' bookshelf in his schoolroom." Jennie shrugged. "I like reading, so I'll look for anything to read."

"I like reading as well." Bryon passed the book back. "I prefer something like *Great Expectations* or *Frankenstein*."

"I've read both of those," Jennie said eagerly. "They're interesting, but I prefer the *Frankenstein* one more. It's something new and fresh." Then she fell silent when she saw Byron's bemusement. "Sorry, I...I shouldn't have spoken out of turn."

"You don't need to be. It's nice to see that you're that interested in reading." Byron tilted his head to one side. "I can see why you were given a chance to pursue your education. There's a passion in your eyes and your words."

"Well..." Jennie licked her lips, clutching the book to her

chest. "I love to learn. It's what gave me an escape from the conditions I was living in. It was solace when my friend died. Everything about it makes me feel like I'm not stupid and worthless."

"Why would you think you're worthless?"

"Because I'm stuck here when I could be with a decent family and not having to worry about when I'm going to be able to eat properly." Jennie couldn't stop herself from talking more. "My parents may have died, but that didn't mean my brother and I should have gotten pushed into an orphanage and forgotten about. I shouldn't have been taken to another workhouse away from him. We should have stayed together, and then maybe we could have made the most of this together." Her throat began to tighten, and she swallowed hard to get rid of it. "Things would be a lot better for me if I had Stephen at my side. I wanted that, and I was lied to so much that I don't know what to believe anymore."

Byron didn't say anything for a moment. He didn't look disgusted by the fact she kept talking and wouldn't stop. If anything, he looked thoughtful. Jennie resisted the urge to squirm. If only he would say something, anything at all. It was building the tension in the air, and she didn't like it.

"You love your brother, don't you?" he asked finally.

"I promised him that I would look after him, and I failed as soon as we got to the orphanage in London. I want to find him again and make sure I'm not going to do that again." She lifted her chin and drew herself up. "I want to work as hard as I can so I know that I can do what I need to do when I can get out of here."

"And if you can't get away from the mill?"

Jennie had never contemplated that. She took a deep breath and let it out slowly.

"That's not an option. I'm going to leave here one of these days. I appreciate Mr Harrison giving myself and Polly a chance to get away from Mr Cooper, but I'm not going to stay here forever. I must get away if I have any chance of getting what I want."

Byron was silent. Jennie knew she had spoken too much, and she turned away, her head bowed.

"I'm sorry, I shouldn't have said anything like that. I'll get back to work."

"Jennie, wait a moment." Byron caught up with her, falling into step as Jennie headed along the river path. "I didn't mean to make you uncomfortable."

"What did you mean to do, then?"

"I just wanted to talk to you, that's all. I've seen how much you work at the mill when I'm visiting, and I'm aware of what Mr Davies is doing. That's a lot to take on for someone of your young age."

Jennie snorted.

"You're not much older than me, Master Byron."

"And even I don't do as much as you do. There is a chance you could overwork yourself and then you would become sick."

"I'm not going to get sick. I've been very lucky with that."

"Are you sure about that?" Byron countered. "There's always a first time, and you are looking exhausted."

Jennie scowled at him.

"You don't need to worry about anything, Master Byron. I can take care of myself."

"I don't doubt that, but won't you let others take care of you."

The sound of that made Jennie bristle. She swung around and glared at him.

"You make it sound like I've got loving people around me to take care of me when I'm all on my own. Sure, I have some friends here, but family?" Jennie blinked back the tears. She wasn't going to cry now. That was not happening. "I only have my brother, but I don't even know if he's alive anymore. It's been almost ten years, and I have no idea where he is. Do you know how hard it is to have that feeling?"

Byron looked sheepish. He cleared his throat.

"I'm an only child," he finally admitted. "I wouldn't know what it's like to be in that position."

"Of course you wouldn't," Jennie scoffed. "You live in a nice house with two parents, you get a good education, and you get things handed to you. Once you're grown up, you don't have to worry about anything else. That's far different to what I have. All I must look forward to if I don't have my motivation is to rot away in the mill carrying flour sacks around or making the bread in the bakery. If I didn't have my education continuing and Mr Davies finally having some faith in me, then I would be stuck."

She was struggling to speak without bursting into tears. Turning away, Jennie hunched her shoulders and bit back a sob. She could feel Byron moving closer, and she flinched.

"I'm sorry, Jennie." He sounded remorseful. "I know this is hard for you..."

"I didn't mean to start getting emotional over this."

"Given what you've been through, I'm not surprised. And I should take it into consideration." Byron paused. "You're smart, I know that much. And Father did well in giving you what you needed to improve yourself. He's never done that with anyone else before."

"Really?" Jennie turned to him. "Why did he do it to me, then?"

"I don't know. Maybe because he saw something in you? He does have a good sense of judgement, so perhaps he thought that he would go with it." Byron managed a small smile. "Some of the workers here have gone on to do other things, I do know that much. If there's a talent, he focuses on it. He's not a bad employer, just strict."

Jennie didn't know if she could argue with that. The conditions in the mill were not that great at all, and the pay she received was barely what she could live on if she didn't live on the property. But it was better than how she had lived as a child. She would take what she could.

"I'm just glad someone felt that I had something to pursue and not stop," she said miserably. "Mr Cooper wanted me to work and not do anything with my books, but Mr Lewis made sure I continued with it whenever I could."

"It's like that when it comes to workhouses. You're supposed to work, not be educated."

"Then what's the point? Aren't we allowed to pursue our dreams?" She pointed at Byron. "You're allowed to go and pursue what you want. So why can't I?"

Byron looked sympathetic, albeit uncomfortable. He nodded at the book in her arms.

"This is your escape, isn't it? It's more than just education. You can get away from what's going on."

Jennie nodded. Mr Lewis had figured that out, and Mr Davies was beginning to see that, too. Now Byron, merely sixteen years old, was seeing the same thing.

"I won't tell Father about this. It's not my place to tell on you when you're doing nothing wrong." Byron tapped the book before lowering his hand. "Just be careful. You know what Father is like when you're not doing what you're supposed to do."

"I'll remember that." Jennie managed a smile. "Thank you, Master Byron."

His smile widened, and Jennie couldn't help but do the same. She didn't think it was possible to have a boy of a completely different social class be so nice, and yet she was grateful for it.

As she walked away, hurrying back to her cottage to hide her book, Jennie looked back at Byron. He was still watching her go, although he seemed to look embarrassed at being caught staring at her before turning away and hurrying out of sight. That made her smile, and her step felt lighter as she walked off.

CHAPTER 9

1867

"Jennie, can you get these over to the main house?" Mrs Tracey said, pointing at the tray of loaves they had just made and were cooling. "Mrs Harrison wants these for her cook. They've got a garden party later today."

"I'll get it sorted, Mrs Tracey." Jennie dusted her hands on her apron before picking up the tray. "Just this one?"

"Just this one for now. Mrs Harrison will let us know if she needs more. Now be off with you."

Jennie's arms barely noticed the strain as she carried the tray out of the kitchen and outside into the sunshine. It was something she had done for a few years already, so the bulky tray was nothing to her. She had been having to deal with it without any complaints. Nobody was going to listen to her. If she did, she would get a scolding and be made to do it even more. Complaining never got anyone anywhere, and Jennie had learned a long time ago that making remarks about how she couldn't do it wasn't going to be listened to.

Mr Harrison might have been a fair employer, but he didn't instil that with the people immediately below him. Jennie wasn't about to make things more complicated for other children by going straight to see Mr Harrison. There were already raised eyebrows that she was still being taught by Mr Davies, so she had to keep her head down.

She made her way over to the Harrison house, wondering if she would see Byron. He was currently at school, but he had told her he would be returning at some point during that week. It was the end of term, and he had one more before he was finished and headed off to university. Jennie felt a little envious that he could do that, and she wasn't allowed, but there was little she could do about it.

She just had to concentrate and work as hard as she could, even if she had no energy for it.

Entering the kitchen, Jennie placed the tray onto the table. The cook wasn't to be seen, and Jennie looked around. There weren't even any of the other kitchen staff around. Where were they?

Perhaps they were in the vegetable garden or out in the market collecting what they needed for the garden party. It was rare to see the place completely empty.

"How's Jennie coming along?"

Jennie jumped. She hadn't anticipated hearing her name coming out of nowhere. It echoed around the room, but there was nobody with her.

If it had been anything else, she would have left the conversation and walked out. She had work to do, after all. But because it was her name, and she recognised Mr Harrison's voice, she was curious. And that piqued when she heard Mr Davies responding.

"She's flourishing, sir. She gets all her work done, and then she helps the smaller children with their schoolwork. I think she could be trained to be a teacher herself. There's that natural ability to help others."

Jennie was surprised at that. Mr Davies didn't praise very often. He was a stoic man who didn't do that much when it

THE ORPHAN JENNIE CLARKE

came to compliments. Did he think that she could be a teacher? She approached the partially open kitchen door and peeked out. Not too far away was Mr Harrison's study, and his door was open. From where she was, Jennie could see Mr Davies back.

"Do you think she should go to normal school, then? I don't want to lose one of my workers, but if she's got the capabilities…"

"I believe she would exceed there, Mr Harrison," Mr Davies replied. "I know you don't want to lose more workers, and she's one of the hardest workers in the mill. But I think Jennie would be more useful becoming a teacher."

"I'll take that into consideration."

"Is there any news about her brother?"

That made Jennie stiffen. She hadn't expected that. Why was Mr Davies bringing up her brother? He was aware that she was looking for him and wanting to find Stephen, but he had never said anything about it."

Mr Harrison sighed.

"That's not something that we should be focusing on."

"Maybe not, but it's the driving force behind her desire," Mr Davies pointed out. "She would be far more productive if she knew that her brother was still alive and well, wouldn't she?"

"That's as may be, but if I did that for Jennie then I would have to look out for every child here. This is a business, not a charity case."

"And yet you went out of your way to agree that I should give her extra lessons when she should be working?"

Jennie knew she should leave this and go back to work, but she wanted to hear what was going on. Why were they talking about her brother? And was Mr Davies standing up for her?

"I probably shouldn't have, but I liked her spirit," Mr Harrison said. "She reminds me a lot of Ellie when we were younger. There's a fire inside her that spoke to me."

"So you decide to help her more because she reminds you of

your wife?" Mr Davies sounded sceptical. "It's not something I expected you to say, if I'm honest."

"Call me soft-hearted, but…I don't know. Maybe I should put that to one side. Although that might be harder to do after all these years." There was the sound of pacing feet. "And I can tell Byron's taken a shine to her."

"Really?"

"I've seen them talking often, and he comes back home more than he used to. All because of her."

Jennie was surprised at that. She hadn't expected him to say that at all. Byron liked her. She was friendly with him, but she was the reason he kept coming back.

"Jennie?"

Jennie bit back a squeak as she spun around and saw Byron entering the kitchen from the outside door. Pressing a hand to her chest as her heart pounded, she leaned against the door.

"Don't scare me like that!" she whispered.

"What are you doing?" Byron frowned. "Aren't you supposed to be at the mill?"

"I…" Jennie moved away from the door and pointed at the bread tray. "I brought that in. Then I heard your father talking…"

"And you eavesdropped, did you?"

Jennie looked away, suddenly embarrassed. She wished she didn't turn into a shivering mess around Byron. But she couldn't help herself. Something about her friend just made her weak at the knees, especially when he smiled at her. It was frustrating and distracted her from their friendship, but there were moments when it was quite sweet.

"Come on," Byron whispered, beckoning her to follow him. "Let's go before you're found. Cook is certainly not going to be happy to find you hovering around in here."

"Where are they?"

"The kitchen staff are in the garden picking what they need for the party, and Cook is with Mother going over the food ideas.

You won't be on your own for long." Byron moved towards the outer door. "Come on, Jennie."

Jennie wanted to stay a bit longer and find out if Mr Harrison really did know more about her brother. Did he know where Stephen was? If he did, then that would be perfect. She would know where to reach out, although she would need to be able to find a way to leave the mill to go looking for him.

If only she was able to leave when she could instead of having to bide her time. With the little pay she got, Jennie knew she couldn't cope unless she had a better job. And with Mr Davies' suggestion that they could send her to normal school instead...

"Jennie!" Byron hissed. "Stop daydreaming and come on! We're going to get caught!"

Jennie hurried to him, surprised when Byron took her hand. He gave her a quick smile before tugging her out of the kitchen and back into the sunshine. The feel of his fingers wrapped around hers almost sent her stumbling, and Jennie had to remember how to work her limbs properly as she hurried along beside him.

Byron was a good friend, but she didn't think she could afford such a distraction. Not until she had found Stephen.

* * *

BOTH WERE out of breath once they reached the river. Byron let go of Jennie's hand and gasped for air, hands on his knees with his body heaving. Jennie couldn't help but laugh at the sight.

"I thought you were supposed to have done some sort of physical education at school."

"We did, but not that much. It's more focused on academics." Byron straightened up; his face flushed from the running. "Maybe I should start doing that soon. That's embarrassing to be out of breath, and we've barely gone anywhere."

"It was your idea to run," Jennie reminded him.

Byron gave her a rueful look.

"How are you not out of breath? You're barely flushed."

Jennie shrugged.

"You work in the place I do where you're always on the go, you get used to it. We don't run, but have you tried carrying heavy bags and trays up several flights of stairs?"

Byron winced.

"I suppose that was a stupid thing to say."

"It's fine. You're not in the same position I am, so it's just something that's there." Jennie wiped the sweat off her forehead and sighed as the breeze wafted past them. "It's such a gorgeous day today, so maybe we should wait here for the moment."

"I guess." Byron collapsed onto the grass. "That's better."

Jennie giggled.

"You just wanted an excuse to sit down, didn't you?"

"Is it that obvious?"

"A little bit." She settled beside him, dusting down her skirts. "I can't stay here for too long, though. Mrs Tracey is going to wonder where I am. I'm sure she'll figure out that I'm with you once she hears you're back."

"Why would she think that?"

"Because you and I are often around each other when you're home, and people have begun to notice." Jennie sighed and shook her head. "I've had a bit of a talking to about it from Mrs Tracey and a few others. Something about I shouldn't be conversing with you so much as it's inappropriate. People are going to think bad things about me, and I need to know my place."

Byron arched an eyebrow.

"Bad things? Like what?"

"Like I'm looking to marry 'up', in their words."

Jennie felt her face getting warm as she said that. She had been shocked when that had been mentioned to her before. She would never have considered that. She was aware that it would never happen, and she hadn't thought about it at all.

Byron was just a friend who had made her feel better when she had a bad day. He had a sense of humour that would lift anyone's spirits. The thought of getting married to him horrified her.

Although not as much as she thought it would. She avoided his surprised stare and plucked at the grass around her.

"They think you're looking to marry out of here?" Byron sounded stunned. "That's ridiculous!"

"I haven't even thought about anything except getting out of here and finding Stephen. That's more important." Jennie bit her lip. "Sorry, I didn't mean to offend…"

"I'm not offended. I would have been if you were thinking of marriage." Byron sat back on his hands. "You're one of the most straightforward people I've ever met, Jennie. You're certainly not a person who would behave in such a manner. Some of the other girls, certainly, but not you."

"I…I don't know what to say to that."

"You don't need to say anything." Byron smiled. "Just be thankful that you're not lumped in with the other girls who try some flirtatious remarks with me."

"Really?"

"People really do that with me. I try to be pleasant and respectful, but there are workers who think they can do that. I must try and extract myself as much as possible."

Jennie was surprised when she felt a surge of jealousy in her chest. She had never felt like that before. She pushed it away and tried to focus on the conversation.

"Sounds like everyone wants to get out of here, then."

"I'm not surprised. The conditions aren't that great, and Father says he's doing his best to improve them, but I'm not seeing it." Byron frowned. "He could, at the very least, pay his workers a little better. It's only fair if they're working for several hours more than they should."

"Why won't he do it?"

"Something about Mother oversees the finances, including the wages from the mill, and she is the one to talk to. It sounds like utter nonsense to pass the blame on why the workers aren't being paid."

Jennie let this sink in. She had thought Mr Harrison was decent enough, and he did seem to care about things when spoken to, but when it came to the wages it was another matter. It was like talking to a brick wall. Why it would be like that, she had no idea.

He was better than Mr Cooper, but it still felt like she was stuck.

"You want to leave here, don't you?" Bryon asked quietly.

Jennie couldn't lie to him. She nodded.

"I've got to find my brother. I need to know where he is."

"I'm sure you'll be able to find him. He's out there somewhere."

"But where? I can't scour the whole of the country looking for him, can I?"

"Maybe you should hire someone to find him?" Byron suggested. "There's always someone who would be able to find anyone."

Jennie scoffed at that.

"I doubt it. That would be expensive. And nobody's going to go looking for an orphaned girl's little brother for free."

"I'm sure you'll be able to find him. Whether he's alive or…" Byron hesitated. "Or dead, there are plenty of records."

Jennie felt a cold shiver down her spine. She knew that there was a possibility that Stephen was dead. But then she reminded herself of the conversation she overheard not too long ago. Her brother was alive, and she had to cling onto that hope.

"I have a bad set of cards for my life, but I'm not about to let it get to me." She picked at the blade of grass between her fingers. "I know it's sounding like I'm making excuses for everything, but when it's stacked against me, what am I supposed to do?"

"Keep fighting." Byron nodded firmly. "You just need to keep fighting. You're a tough girl, Jennie, and I know you can do it."

Jennie peered at him curiously.

"Why do you have such faith in me, Byron? Your father sees some potential in me, but I don't think he has much faith in my abilities."

"What makes you think that?"

"It's the way he talks about me, I guess. I don't know." Jennie slumped back and laid down on the grass, staring up at the bright blue sky. "There are days when I'm just so fed up with all of this. I don't know what I'm saying anymore. It's like my mind is going around in circles."

"It sounds like it, if I'm honest." Byron leaned back and propped himself up on his elbow. "And I get that. You're really trying to go one way, but you're being tugged in different directions. It's far too much for you, and you feel like you're going mad."

Jennie felt a bit of tension leave her body. He understood her more than she anticipated. Polly and Emma understood her, especially Polly, but then there was Byron. In the years since she had come to work at the flour mill, she was surprised at Byron's friendliness and his kindness. They could spend hours talking to each other, but it had to be snatched moments with everyone watching them closely.

Why couldn't she have more freedom? It was not easy at all. The only way she would have any freedom was if she got away from the mill.

She had to focus on the chances she was given, otherwise she was never going anywhere.

"You also need to stop thinking too much, Jennie," Byron continued, pressing a finger to the middle of her forehead. "That's what is giving you those pains in the head. You think far too much on what you're doing, and you need to just close your eyes and forget about things for a while."

Jennie snorted.

"How am I supposed to do that?"

"Just by some deep breathing and counting to ten."

"Are you serious about that?"

Byron smiled.

"That's one way of doing it. It works with me. And if you give it a chance, it will help you, too."

Jennie doubted that it would, but she would try anything to make herself feel better. She was about to respond to him when she heard Mrs Harrison calling from the house far away.

"Byron? Byron, where are you?"

Byron sighed and began to get to his feet. Jennie felt her heart sinking. This meant she was on her own, that she would have to go back to work. And she didn't want Byron to leave.

"I'd better get back before Mother realises what I'm doing." He held out a hand to her. "And you need to return, otherwise you're going to end up having questions asked about your whereabouts."

Jennie huffed, but she took his hand and allowed him to pull her to her feet.

"I wish I didn't have to."

"Things will get better, Jennie." Byron squeezed her hand. "Just take it one day at a time. You'll get what you want eventually."

Jennie was so stunned by the tingling sensation in her fingers from Byron's grip that she didn't know what to say in return. She could only watch Byron as he walked away, feeling like she was getting a little cold in the warm afternoon.

CHAPTER 10

868

"Jennie!" Polly ran into the bakery, her hair flying behind her and bringing up a cloud of flour as she practically slammed her hands onto the table. "Jennie, you won't believe who's just come here!"

Mrs Tracey frowned at her as she lifted two more tins into the oven.

"Polly, could you go and get on with your work? Things are going to get behind if you keep running around."

"Yes, Mrs Tracey." Polly barely acknowledged her, focusing on Jennie as her friend kneaded the dough. "You've got to come and see this! I can't believe it!"

Jennie frowned. Polly was perfectly giddy, something she hadn't seen in a long time. Her eyes were shining, and she was jumping up and down, almost as if she was seeing Christmas for the first time.

"What's gotten into you, Polly? Why are you like this?"

"Come and find out! You're going to be so surprised!" Polly reached over and grabbed at Jennie's wrist. "Come on, now!"

"But..."

"Polly!" Mrs Tracey admonished. "Would you stop it and get back to your work? What...?"

She didn't get any further before Jennie was being practically dragged out of the bakery. She could hardly stop herself when Polly was this excited. Her friend was like a force to be reckoned with when she was behaving this way. Jennie gave Mrs Tracey an apologetic look before she was tugged out of the room and into the autumn afternoon. It was warmer than usual, with the leaves turning dark red and orange, crunching underfoot as the girls ran through them.

Byron was talking to his father near the main gate into the courtyard. For a moment, Jennie thought Polly was going a little mad, but then she saw the other young man standing with them. He was tall and handsome, dressed well like Byron and Mr Harrison, looking confident and proud. There was something very familiar about him, but Jennie couldn't place him.

Then his face turned towards her as he answered something Byron asked, and she realised who it was. And she couldn't believe her eyes.

"Is that...?"

"It's him!" Polly squeaked. "It's Maurice!"

Jennie couldn't believe it. It had been close to eight years since they last saw Maurice when his father sent him away to a school on the other side of the country, and now he was right in front of them.

How was that even possible?

Mr Harrison said something to his son and Maurice before walking away. Byron caught sight of Jennie first, and he grinned. He was clearly up to something. Then he whispered to Maurice, nodding in the girls' direction. Maurice turned, blinking in surprise when he saw them. Jennie saw recognition dawning, his eyes widening.

"I can't believe it's really him," Polly breathed. "I thought we'd never see him again."

"Neither did I. Didn't Mr Cooper make sure he could never come back?"

Before Polly could reply, the two young men approached them. Maurice looked slightly awkward as he looked Polly, but he smiled and that lit up his whole face.

"Now there is a sight for sore eyes."

Polly didn't say anything. Instead, she launched herself at him and flung her arms around his neck. Maurice coughed and almost stumbled, but then he put his arms around Polly and hugged her back in return. He let out a sigh of relief.

"You have no idea how glad I am to see you two." He eased Polly back and looked her up and down. "I can't believe the two of you are here. You're looking well, Polly."

Polly's cheeks went a little pink and she suddenly became quite coy, something Jennie noticed quickly. Her friend bit her lip and gestured at herself.

"I wouldn't say I'm well, but I'm still alive."

"That's something, anyway." Maurice turned to Jennie. "Jennie."

"Maurice." Jennie hugged him, surprised at how tall he was. "I think the last time I saw you; you were about my height."

Maurice chuckled.

"We're all grown up now. Now I'm at university and sharing a room with Byron." He gestured at the other young man, who simply shrugged. "He told me about the mill, and then he started talking about you."

"Me?" Jennie squeaked.

"As soon as I heard more, I knew it had to be you. And once I heard Polly was here as well, I had to come here and see it for myself."

Jennie stared at Byron, who didn't meet her gaze. He looked slightly bashful. Polly looked excited, still staring at Maurice with adoration in her eyes.

"I thought we'd never see you again," she said. "When your father sent you away…"

Maurice grinned.

"You can't get rid of me that easily, Polly. I wouldn't let that happen."

"Jennie! Polly!" Mrs Tracey appeared in the courtyard behind them. She didn't look happy, her hands on her hips. "You need to get back to work right now! You weren't meant to relinquish your duties. Get back to it!"

Jennie sighed and tugged on her friend's arm.

"Come on, we've got to do as we're told. We can't stand here behaving like this."

Polly pouted, but she allowed Jennie to pull her away. She gave Maurice an apologetic look.

"Sorry. We can't do anything about it."

"I know." Maurice's expression softened. "I'll be staying with Byron for a while. I'll see you soon."

Polly beamed, and Jennie had to tug her away so she would start walking. Her friend stumbled, but she followed her.

"What's gotten into you?" Jennie whispered as they followed Mrs Tracey back to the mill. "You're suddenly going weak-kneed about Maurice?"

"I didn't mean to!" Polly protested. "But there's something about him that makes my heart skip, and I feel like I'm fresh and happy for the first time."

Jennie arched an eyebrow at her.

"What? What are you saying? You find Maurice attractive?"

"Don't you?"

Jennie could admit Maurice had grown into a good-looking man, but she didn't see him that way. She had known him as a child, and the idea of being attracted to him was just strange. Something she would never contemplate, but Polly didn't seem to have the same thought.

"I've never seen him like that. I was a lot younger than you when he left, remember?"

Polly giggled and nudged Jennie.

"Well, you wouldn't want your attention away from your Byron, would you?"

"What are you talking about? My Byron?"

"Come on, Jennie. Everyone's noticed that you and Byron Harrison are close. You spend a lot of time together. People are beginning to talk about it."

Jennie frowned, even though she knew it to be true.

"What do you mean?"

"That you might be taking advantage of him."

Jennie stopped and gave her a look of stunned amazement. Polly winced.

"I'm sorry, Jennie. I didn't want to say that to you, and I know you would never do that, but that's what people are thinking."

Jennie sighed. It should have been expected, given that she did spend a lot of time talking to Byron. She hadn't thought anyone would care. They had to know that she was a person who wouldn't put herself in that sort of position.

Maybe she had without realising it.

"Oh, Jennie." Polly slipped an arm around her shoulders. "Don't think about it that way. Ignore them. Just keep being yourself. I know you can rise head and shoulders above them."

"But what if the rumours keep building and I end up with a reputation that I never wanted?"

"If they've got nothing better to do than to start something stupid, then let them. You carry on. You're not doing anything wrong. I know you're not."

Jennie liked that she had a friend on her side. She needed that.

* * *

"Did you know that Polly and Maurice had a friendship like this when you were children?" Byron asked Jennie as they walked along the river.

Jennie scoffed.

"Of course not. I was small when we all knew each other. I wouldn't have known anything different."

"It looks like they're old lovers reconnecting."

Jennie gasped.

"Don't say that, Byron! If your father finds out what's going on…"

"It's nothing to do with him. If Maurice and Polly want to explore their friendship further, why shouldn't they?" Byron shrugged. "It's not really up to us if they should or shouldn't if they like each other."

Jennie gave him a bemused smile.

"Are you playing matchmaker with them, Byron?"

"Me? Whatever would give you that impression?"

He gave her a wink and then turned to look at Polly and Maurice further along the path. They had finished their shift at the mill, and Byron suggested chaperoning each other as they went for a walk. Even though Polly and Maurice seemed more interested in talking to each other. Jennie wondered what Mr Harrison was going to say when he found out his son and his friend were talking to a couple of girls at the mill. He certainly wasn't going to be impressed.

She needed to stop thinking about what Polly told her earlier. It was not going to help her mood right now.

"I still can't believe that you and Maurice ended up sharing a room at university," she said, watching as Polly touched Maurice's arm as she talked, resulting in a smile from the young man. "It feels like one of the most unlikely things that could possibly have happened."

"I know that, and I was shocked when Maurice told me about

where he grew up in, and that he knew you as well." Byron paused. "He was sent away by his father because he was friendly with your lot, wasn't he?"

Jennie nodded.

"We never got the answer for it, but we suspected it was because he was our friend. He didn't like how his father treated us, and he would stand up to him. Then…" She took a deep breath. Even after all this time, it still hurt to think about. "Then our friend William died. He was very sick, and he just…passed away during a cold winter. Maurice comforted us and was at our side when we buried him. His father, Mr Cooper, was furious that he was there, and he forbade him from coming around us. But when Maurice ignored that, he was sent away for school instead of having a tutor. We didn't think we would ever see him again."

"And what was Polly's reaction?"

"She was devastated. I think, even back then, she was close to Maurice." Jennie watched Polly; her face lit up with her joy. "I can tell she's delighted to see him. I just didn't expect it to be that much."

"Well, you're seeing it now."

Jennie couldn't help but glance over her shoulder at the mill close by. Some of the workers were heading over to their cottages while others were coming in and out, carrying sacks of flour. Some of them were going to be watching them. There was no hiding, even if they were behaving properly. She felt a shiver up her spine, sure that someone was paying attention and wondering if she and Polly were behaving inappropriately.

"What's wrong, Jennie?"

"Hmm?"

Byron nudged her.

"You've been rather skittish since you left the mill. Is something wrong?"

Jennie hesitated. Should she tell him about what Polly had told her? It might result in Byron distancing himself from her, and she didn't want that. For the first time in her life, she wanted to be selfish for herself.

"Jennie?" Byron prompted. "You don't need to hide anything from me. I'll find out sooner or later."

Jennie sighed. She wouldn't be able to keep it from him for much longer. He would find out sooner or later.

"Like I mentioned before, I'm worried about people thinking that we're doing something we shouldn't."

Byron arched an eyebrow.

"Like what? We're not exactly being inappropriate, are we?"

"Do you think anyone is going to agree with that?" Jennie brushed her hair away from her face, tucking it behind her ears. "Polly said that people are talking about you and I and our friendship. About how I must be…well…"

She couldn't say it, that was too embarrassing. But Byron finished the sentence for her.

"They think that you're trying to further your position by cosying up to me, correct?"

Jennie flinched. Byron sighed.

"They're just looking for something exciting to make their lives more interesting, and that includes gossiping about other people."

"And you're not worried about it?"

"Why would I? We're just friends talking with each other, and nothing's happened that could be considered inappropriate. If they want to cause trouble for others, then let them. We know we haven't done anything wrong."

Jennie didn't know how to react to that. Byron may not be upset about it, but she was. It wouldn't fade away from her mind knowing that someone could be whispering about them right now.

Again, she glanced back towards the mill. Was someone watching them or was that her imagination? She needed to stop being so anxious, but that wasn't easy.

"Jennie." Byron laid a hand on her back. "You need to stop thinking so much. It's going to give you a headache, and you won't be able to focus properly."

"Now you're beginning to sound like a parent," Jennie grumbled.

Byron chuckled.

"It's something my grandfather used to say to me when I was small. Apparently, I used to frown a lot."

"I don't doubt that," Jennie giggled. "Why were you frowning so much?"

"I was just a child who worried a lot. And I still do. Mainly about this place." Byron gestured at the mill, poking through the trees behind them. "Father and Grandpa told me that this would be the perfect thing to bring in the money and make us wealthy, but while they are decent people they don't completely care about the overall effects on the workers. They're struggling, and it's clear to me."

Jennie knew that much. She was experiencing it herself. While it was better than where she had been before, it was still dire.

"Why don't they make something of it? And if they don't care about the workers, why is Mr Harrison agreeing to send me to normal school? If he didn't care, he wouldn't do that."

Byron paused. He glanced at Maurice and Polly, who were still in deep conversation further ahead, although they had stopped walking. Then he turned to Jennie and lowered his voice.

"I think it's because you and I are spending time together, and he doesn't like that."

"What?"

"I come back from school because I want to see you, Jennie.

And I spend a lot of time around you instead of my family, and my parents have noticed." Byron sheepishly rubbed the back of his neck. "I've had a few conversations with them about me spending time with one of the workers, and I don't listen to them."

Jennie's mouth fell open.

"Really? I didn't know they'd spoken to you about me."

"They thought I should be interacting with those who are of our own social class." Byron rolled his eyes. "I told them they were behaving senselessly. What's wrong with being friends with another person? I don't care if the other person is respectful. What's the point of being around someone when they don't treat you well?"

He had a very good point, and Jennie didn't know how to respond to that. She felt a stab of guilt knowing that Mr and Mrs Harrison weren't happy with their friendship and wanted them to stop. And that Mr Harrison might use sending her to normal school to get her away from Byron? She wasn't sure how she felt about that now.

"Byron!"

Byron groaned and turned around. Mrs Harrison was walking towards them, her skirts swishing around her legs as she strode sharply towards them. Her expression was not one that showed her pleasure. Jennie wanted to run the other way seeing that.

"What is it, Mother?" Byron called back.

"You and Maurice need to come back to the house. It's almost time for dinner." Mrs Harrison's frown deepened when she saw Maurice further down the path. "What do you think you're doing?"

"We'll be right with you." Byron turned to Jennie and gave her a sheepish smile. "Will you and Polly be all right on your own?"

"Of course. And I'm sorry that I'm causing some conflict within your family."

He didn't respond, but something in his eyes softened. Jennie thought he was going to reach out and touch her for a split second, but then he abruptly moved away from her and beckoned Maurice over. As the two young men convened and talked, Polly joined Jennie and watched the scene nervously.

"We're not going to get into trouble, are we?"

"I don't think so."

Although Jennie wasn't entirely sure, especially with the way Mrs Harrison was looking at her. She didn't look too impressed.

It felt like she was being tugged in different directions. Jennie wanted to get the money she could squirrel away so she could leave and find her brother, but also, she desired to go to normal school, get a good position with better pay and use that to search for Stephen.

Either way, her motivation to get out and away from the mill was strong. But when people kept throwing things up in the way of what she wanted, Jennie didn't know what to do. It felt like she had been thrown into the river to swim on her own without any help, and she was just about keeping her head above water.

At least Byron was around. He was keeping her sane despite everything. If he wasn't here, Jennie didn't think she would be able to cope as well as she was.

As Byron and Maurice walked by, Byron glanced over at her, and their eyes met. Jennie felt her heart leap and stutter in her chest, and her mouth went dry. She couldn't stop herself from staring, especially when he gave her a smile before moving on. That had been happening a lot lately, and Jennie didn't know what was going on there. Whatever it was, it was intense.

Then she saw Mrs Harrison watching her and she grabbed Polly's hand.

"We'd better get back to the cottage," she mumbled. "We don't have a lot of time before we have to go back to work."

"It's a shame we can't have a day off," Polly sighed.

Jennie couldn't agree more. She needed time to settle things in her head and wonder if she was going to have more happy moments like when she saw Maurice for the first time in years. That was one bright part of her life.

Another was Byron. He certainly made things better whenever he was around. Jennie could only hope that she didn't have that taken away from her.

CHAPTER 11

1869

It was still pitch-black when Jennie left the cottage, the cold autumn air rippling around her. It went down the collar of her coat, making her shiver. She was tempted to go back into the house, but knowing she was meeting someone was enough to get her moving.

This was daring. If she got caught, she would get into trouble. But with the Harrison household fast asleep and the night-shift workers in the mill, busy getting the bread ready, there was hopefully going to be nobody around to question what she was up to. Jennie didn't want to explain herself, either.

Even so, she felt like someone was watching her as she hurried along the path, heading towards the gate that led her into Houghton itself. She had to meet at the village square and, hopefully, the money she had would be enough for what she needed. It had taken several weeks to get someone to agree to meet her, and she couldn't let this fail now.

It took all of her savings, but Jennie knew it would be worth it.

"What on earth are you doing?"

Jennie let out a scream and spun around, slamming into a hard body right behind her. She continued to scream, but a hand was put over her mouth.

"Calm down! It's only me!" Byron's voice reached her ears. "Jennie, stop! Someone's going to see us!"

Jennie froze, and he used that moment to take his hand away. She stared at him, his face still bathed in shadow and trying to ignore the fact she was pressed up against his chest with his arms around her.

"Byron? What are you doing awake at this time of the morning?"

"I was going to ask you the same thing."

"I asked first."

Byron sighed.

"I couldn't sleep, so I thought I'd go for a walk, and then I saw you walking away from the cottages. What are you up to?"

Jennie gulped. She should trust him on this, but there was still a part of her that stopped. He was going to tell her this was stupid, and she shouldn't do it.

However, he was her friend. And she should be able to trust him. Jennie bit her lip.

"I was going to meet someone I've been...well..."

"What?" Byron sounded confused. "What are you saying, Jennie?"

"I've been asking for someone to look for Stephen. I'm going to meet them tonight to pay him."

She didn't need to see his face to know that Byron looked shocked. He shifted and then moonlight fell across his face. Sure enough, he looked stunned.

"You're actually sneaking away to pay someone you've hired to look for your brother?"

"Yes. I need to know where he is, and your father isn't going to tell me." Jennie shook her head. "I'm fed up with being stuck in a position where I don't know what's going on. I'm taking charge of it now."

"But…do you know that this could be dangerous for you, don't you? If you don't know the man and haven't met him in person, he could be taking advantage of you."

"I've got to do it, Byron," Jennie protested, lowering her voice when she realised it was rising. She didn't want to draw further attention to herself. "I need to do something. What do you expect me to do? Work here for the rest of my life and twiddle my thumbs?"

"But aren't you heading off to normal school in a few weeks? That's your escape, isn't it?"

Jennie didn't want to think about it that way. Not when it meant leaving Byron as well. She stepped out of his arms, noticing that he seemed reluctant to let her go.

"I've used what I've saved over the last year to pay this man," she said stiffly, straightening up even as she shivered in the cold wind. "Nothing matters but finding Stephen. Once I know where he is and that he's been taken care of properly, I'll feel better about things. Until then, I can't leave here without knowing something." She blinked back the tears that were threatening to fall. "Everything has been a mess since I was six years old. All I've wanted is my brother back. Now I have a chance to get that, and I'm not about to back away."

"Jennie…"

"Byron, you know how much I want to find my brother. Stephen matters to me, and I've been lied to so much it's ridiculous. I need to do this for my own sanity. If I still have a chance to leave, then I leave, but wanting to know where Stephen is won't go away. The sooner I know where he is, the better I'll feel."

Byron sighed and ran his fingers through his hair.

"I understand that…"

"Then please don't stop me. I know this is rather questionable, but it's what I need to do. I've got my money ready to pay him, and I won't be deterred."

Jennie was aware of the problems meeting a man she had only corresponded with through letters in the middle of the night, but she was desperate. "

Mr Cooper had promised to bring Stephen to me, and he didn't do that. Your father knows that he's alive, but he refuses to tell me anything. He might be a fairer employer than what I had before, but he's not a good man because he doesn't truly care, and you know that. I must do this myself."

Her throat hurt from saying all of that, and Jennie felt like she was going to burst into tears again. She couldn't do that; she had more important things to do. Finally, Byron held up his hands.

"All right. Would it make you feel better if I went with you?"

"What?"

"I won't stop you if this is what you want to do, but I'm not about to let you go alone. Not when it's too dangerous. So I'll come with you now, and I'll be there when you meet with him."

Jennie felt like she was still asleep, and she was dreaming this. Did Byron just say he would accompany her? She spluttered.

"I…well…are you sure?"

Byron snorted.

"What sort of friend would I be if I didn't make sure you were safe? You're certainly not sneaking away in the middle of the night alone, to do that."

Jennie stared at him. That was his protective side all over. He was always wanting to do something for her, and that had never stopped over the years. She wanted to throw her arms around his neck and kiss him, but she stopped herself.

Pushing aside her shock, she managed a nod.

"All right. You can come with me. But don't make things more uncomfortable for me, please? I don't want this to go wrong."

"Of course not." He held up his hands. "I'm not about to do that to you, Jennie."

Jennie believed him. Byron had not let her down before. Her heart swelled knowing that he was going to be there for her. He didn't have to do that, but he was always there when she needed him.

She couldn't help but feel a lighter tread in her step as she walked away, Byron following her silently.

* * *

THE GENTLEMAN JENNIE had found who said he would look for Stephen was waiting where they agreed, sitting in the shadows and making himself inconspicuous. It made Jennie nervous and, for the first time, glad that Byron had come along with her. She couldn't believe she thought that this would work on her own. That was just asking for trouble.

But Byron was there. He hung back, watching out for her as Jennie spoke to the gentleman and gave him her savings. The man promised to find what he could, and he would update her in a month. That was all Jennie could afford. She would have to do something drastic to ask for more, but this was her only hope right now. She had to believe this could work.

Thirteen years without seeing her little brother, and she couldn't wait any longer. It had been her driving motivation all this time, and it would be foolish to step away now.

When the gentleman disappeared, Byron joined Jennie as she sagged onto a bench with a heavy sigh.

"That went better than I thought it would," he remarked.

"It did. I just hope I can get something out of it and he wasn't conning me out of my money."

"And if he was?"

Jennie shuddered. She didn't want to think about that. Byron settled beside her.

"Look, if you want, if you need money to find your brother, I can help you."

"What?" Jennie thought she had misheard. She stared at him. "What did you say? You would help me?"

"Of course. I would help my friends with anything they wanted. And that includes you." Byron snorted as if he thought her question was stupid to voice out loud. "You think that I wouldn't help you?"

"But...what about your parents? Surely, you wouldn't be able to help me out without them knowing about it."

"Trust me, I will do whatever you need. You deserve this, Jennie, and I want to see you smile more." Byron sat back on the bench and looked around. "Let's put it this way, I would find it nothing short of a miracle if anyone working at the mill smiled about their life right now. It's just heartbreaking to see."

Jennie had heard Byron talk about it before, and she knew what he meant. Conditions were rough and the hours were long. It was surprising that was the case considering they did well and the money that came in was a lot. Enough that Byron could live in a big house with his family and a household staff as well as go to a boarding school and university.

His world was the complete opposite to what she had grown up in, and yet there was a humbleness about him that brought him back down to earth. It was quite nice to see.

"But there isn't much we can do," she said, turning the collar of her coat up. "I know that a few of the workers in the mill itself have complained about the conditions and want things to be changed, but it doesn't happen at the speed that we want it. It's almost like we're being placated and then it doesn't happen."

The more she talked, the more she had the realisation that Mr Harrison wasn't as good as she thought he was. He promised things and never followed through. It was never going to happen.

"I'm due to inherit the mill once Father decides to pass it on or he passes away," Byron said quietly. "And I intend to change things."

"How so?"

"Like making sure conditions are as good as production. Listening to what the workers want and looking after their needs." Byron nodded as if he was talking to himself. "You look after your workers; they'll look after you. Productivity is better as well, and it makes everything good for all parts of the line, from the youngest to the oldest worker."

Jennie had heard Byron mention things like this before, but he hadn't talked about when he took over. His father was a relatively healthy man, so she didn't see him passing away or giving charge of the mill over to his son anytime soon. However, it was nice to hear that Byron had plans for the place that would benefit other people.

"Do you think you'll be able to enforce what you want?" she asked. "There are some people still loyal to your father, and I don't know if they'll allow it."

Byron snorted.

"It'll happen. Trust me. I've witnessed this all my life, and I know what I need to do to change it. I'm not about to back down because of a few stupid people too stubborn to change themselves."

There was a lot of passion in his voice, and Jennie liked it. That was something she and Byron had in common: they shared a passion for what they wanted in life. They were in different walks of life and their social standings were very different as well, but when it came down to it the two of them were the same.

On impulse, she leaned over and kissed his cheek. Byron started.

"What was that for?"

"That was to thank you for being there for me. For looking out for me when you didn't need to."

Byron stared at her. Then he smiled and leaned in to kiss her head, putting an arm around her shoulders.

"I'll do whatever you want, Jennie. Anything for you. Just make sure you know that."

Jennie felt warmth spread through her stomach when she heard that. That was the sweetest thing anyone had ever said to her. She felt blessed hearing it. She smiled back.

"I appreciate that, Byron."

An awkward silence fell between them, and Jennie was very aware of how close to Byron she was, leaning against his side. Then Byron stood up abruptly and tugged her to her feet.

"Let's get back. You haven't got long before you've got to get to work, and I bet you have had little sleep."

"Not much," Jennie admitted.

"Then you'd better put your head down for a while." He squeezed her hand. "I'll walk you back. And please make sure you let me know in the future. I don't want you walking around at night on your own. Promise me you won't do that again."

"I promise."

As far as she was concerned, Jennie would never do that again.

CHAPTER 12

"Well, well. Look who it is. I see that things never change with you. Still reading books as if that's more important than anything else."

Jennie froze. She couldn't believe her ears. That voice had to be coming from her head, surely. She had been so engrossed in her book that she had started hearing things.

But when she looked up, she saw Mr Cooper leaning against a nearby tree, watching her with a smirk but no mirth on his face. Slamming her book shut, Jennie jumped to her feet.

"Mr Cooper." She hated that her heart started racing at the sight of the man. "What are you doing here?"

"I heard some shocking news about my son. Something about him spending time with a factory girl instead of furthering our family's connections. Especially now I'm on the board for this mill."

"What?"

"I'm part of the group of people who make decisions about what happens at this mill." Mr Cooper scoffed at her. "Did you think that this place was solely run by Mr Harrison? Even he needs financial backing to have it going as it does."

Jennie couldn't believe this was happening. She had hoped she would never see this man again, not after the way he had treated her.

"Why would you do that?" she asked, her voice trembling. "I thought you were in charge of that place in Surrey."

"I still am, but I took up Mr Harrison's generous offer to be one of his financial backers, now that things have improved on my end." Mr Cooper ran a hand over his greying hair. He looked like he was preening. "I've made things quite successful, if I say so myself."

"Then why are you wasting your time bothering me?" Jennie snapped. "Don't you have better things to do?"

If it had been anyone else, she would have remembered her manners and kept her voice to herself. But this was the man who abused so many children, including her, and she had a personal hatred for this man who lied to her. She wasn't about to back down now, glaring back at him. Mr Cooper raised an eyebrow.

"You've gotten quite insolent now, haven't you?"

"I'm nineteen now, Mr Cooper. I'm not a child anymore. You're not going to frighten me."

"Am I not? Even though I can ruin you?"

Jennie snorted at that.

"I'm a factory girl. Do you really think that's going to scare me?"

Mr Cooper looked her up and down. Jennie didn't like it, and she resisted the urge to squirm. Even after years away from him, he still scared her. She wasn't about to back down from her stance, though.

She just wanted him to leave her alone.

"You mean I can't go around saying that you're being…inappropriate with a certain young man who happens to be the son of your employer?"

"What are you talking about?"

"Everyone knows about you and Byron Harrison. People have

been…implying that something more than friendship is happening."

Jennie rolled her eyes. She knew all about that.

"They're just bored and looking for something to gossip about. Byron and I are friends, and there's nothing inappropriate going on."

"That's not what others think. And Mr Harrison has heard about the rumours himself. He's not happy about it at all. As for his wife…" Mr Cooper exaggerated a shudder. "She certainly hates that you're dragging their precious boy down just by associating with him. No matter what they say, Byron won't even listen to him. Just like my Maurice." His lip curled in a snarl. "Imagine how I felt when I received word that he kept coming here instead of returning home for the holidays to spend time with a girl named Polly. Your friend, am I right? Both of you are not much less than harlots."

Jennie gasped. She couldn't believe what she was hearing.

"How dare you? We're just spending time with friends!"

"You mean you're trying to get something better than what you've got right now? I know that Maurice is thinking about asking Polly to marry him."

"Excuse me?"

"You didn't know?" Mr Cooper sniggered. "As if it's going to happen. My wife and I aren't going to approve of him marrying an orphan factory girl. He'll be disowned, and he knows it. But he's so stubborn it's just ridiculous."

Jennie was still reeling from the news that Maurice was going to propose to Polly. She hadn't anticipated that, although she should have expected it with the way Maurice looked at her friend. Those two were blossoming in their romance, and it was adorable. To have Mr Cooper ruin that for them would be heartbreaking.

"Don't you want your son to be happy?" she protested. "If he loves someone, then why not let him go through with it? You wouldn't want him married to someone he doesn't love because he's trying to be a part of your ridiculous standards?"

The man's eyes narrowed, and Jennie stopped herself from taking a step back. Even though she was grown, Mr Cooper still scared her. Her heart was racing so fast that she felt light-headed. Mr Cooper stepped towards her.

"He is our son, and he will do what is best for the family. Marrying a harlot orphan is not acceptable. He'll understand that soon. As for you…don't expect to be working here any longer with Mr and Mrs Harrison angry that you're spending time with their son."

"Nobody's going to send me away for being friends with someone!"

"You think so? All I have to do is say I know what your reputation was like when you were at my factory…"

Jennie's stomach dropped. She couldn't believe what she was hearing.

"What? You mean when I was a small child? How is that going to work?"

"Harlots work at a young age, don't they?" Mr Cooper sniggered. "I said nothing to Mr Harrison at the time as I wanted to get rid of you, but if…"

Jennie felt sick. He will spread vicious lies to ruin her? She had never seen such animosity towards a child.

"Why do you hate me so much?" she asked. "What did I ever do to you? I was six years old when you met me. How can you have so much hatred towards a child who can't do anything to you?"

Mr Cooper shrugged.

"There's something about you I don't like. I don't need a reason more than that."

"That sounds like the most pathetic thing I've ever heard." Jennie didn't want to hear anything more. She turned away. "Good day, Mr Cooper."

"Where do you think you're going?" he demanded. "We haven't finished talking!"

"We weren't talking to begin with, and I'm not about to stand there and listen to you discredit someone you've declared you hated *as a child*." Jennie barely glanced over her shoulder. "If you want to be petty about something I had no control of, go right ahead. But I'm not about to listen to any of it."

"Get back here!"

But Jennie simply hurried her pace. She wanted to get away from him before anything further happened. She wasn't about to let the man see her break down. It felt like she was going to faint.

Of all the times for Mr Cooper to turn up, why did it have to be now?

* * *

"Just one thing before you go, Jennie."

Jennie looked up as she put away the book into the desk she had been sitting at. Mr Davies stood up from his desk at the front of the room and approached her. She was surprised by the look on his face. The normally stern man appeared to be worried. That got Jennie's attention.

Something had to be wrong for Mr Davies to look this perturbed.

"Is something the matter, sir?" she asked.

"Well…" Mr Davies hesitated. "I received word from Mr Harrison today. He said to withdraw your application to normal school."

"What?" Jennie thought she must have misheard. "What are you talking about?"

"It was still being looked at, and Mr Harrison told me today to write to the school and say that you're withdrawing."

Jennie's jaw dropped, and she closed her mouth quickly, but it happened again. She had to be in some sort of dream still. The promise of getting away from the mill had been her driving force with her studies, and now it was being snatched away from her.

"But why? He was supportive of furthering me before. Why now?"

"Because he's heard about some...activities that you've been doing while you're here." Mr Davies cleared his throat. "Something about taking money for..."

Jennie didn't need him to finish that sentence. She knew exactly what he meant. Horror and outrage took over.

"He heard what? Why would he believe such lies about me? He should know I wouldn't do that!"

"Well, his opinion changed when Mr Cooper went to him with some concerns about you, and that you were trying to seduce his son as well."

Jennie's legs were shaking, and she had to sit down. Only yesterday, Mr Cooper had said he would drop a few hints about her past, and he would be believed over her. He had followed through on his threat.

She should have been more concerned about it.

"I can't believe it. He's withdrawing me from the school because of some lies Mr Cooper made up?"

"Apparently, he doesn't want the reputation of the school to be ruined by you." Mr Davies held up a hand. "Don't worry, I don't believe anything about this. You're far too strait-laced to do something as despicable as that."

"I'm not sure if that was a compliment, sir."

"I just know it's not you. You're either working or studying. I've not seen anyone with as much dedication as you when it comes to your education."

At least someone believed her. But it didn't stop the nausea forming in her stomach. She felt like she was being pushed underwater, and she couldn't get herself to break away and swim off. She swallowed, trying to stop from panicking.

All she had cared about for years was getting out of the

factory and doing something else. This had been her chance. And now it was being taken away from her.

"You're going to need to come with me, Jennie," Mr Davies said, abruptly moving towards the door.

"Pardon?"

"Just get moving. We haven't got much time."

Confused, Jennie managed to get to her feet and stumbled after him. The teacher's huge stride was enough that she had to run just to keep up. As they left the schoolhouse and crossed the field behind the building towards the gate, she wondered what was going on. What was Mr Davies up to? Why did she need to go with him?

It wasn't until she got to the gate that Jennie saw they weren't alone. Byron, Maurice, and Polly were waiting there, huddled together. Polly had a bag slung over her shoulder, and even in profile Jennie could see she was close to tears. Byron saw the approaching pair first and left the group to join Mr Davies.

"Thank you for doing this, Mr Davies."

"I hope I will not lose my job for this," the schoolteacher muttered.

"Trust me, if anyone finds out what we've done, I won't be saying a word about you." Byron looked at Jennie, his eyes showing his pain. "I'm sorry this is happening to you, Jennie. I had no idea this we'd be doing this."

"What's going on, Byron?" Jennie demanded. "Why are we out here?"

"We're getting you out of here."

"Pardon?"

Byron gestured at Maurice. Then Jennie noticed the horse and cart on the path, patiently waiting. Polly let out a slight whimper, and Maurice's arms tightened around her.

"Mr Cooper is making salacious remarks about you and Polly and your supposed...activities." Byron scowled. "Mother and

Father believe them, despite seeing things for themselves. So we're doing what we can to protect you from it."

"By what?"

"Sending you two away," Mr Davies said grimly. "These two are going to take you girls elsewhere and set you up with a new life. If you stay, your reputations are going to worsen, and when that happens..."

Jennie didn't need him to finish that sentence. She had witnessed that over the years with other young women who associated with someone they shouldn't. Even if it was an innocent interaction, it ended up with them being harassed and more when it was misconstrued. Jennie knew she and Polly wouldn't be able to cope with that if it turned on them.

"Mr Cooper is horrible," Polly said, her voice thick with emotion. "We were children, and he would rather ruin us because we're friends with Maurice and Byron."

"Father's always been a bully," Maurice said darkly. He rubbed Polly's back. "I won't let him hurt you, Polly. I would never let you suffer."

"Same here." Byron never took his eyes off Jennie. "We'll do whatever we can to protect you."

Jennie didn't know what to say to that. Mr Davies huffed and looked over his shoulder.

"Would you stop with the sappy talk and get a move on? I want to remain ignorant about this, so I shouldn't be caught out here."

"We'll be going as soon as possible, Mr Davies," Byron promised. He held out a hand to Jennie. "Are you coming? If you stay, you know things are going to get worse."

Jennie hesitated. She was still coming to terms with the fact they were running away. Her mind was reeling from the news.

"Are you sure this is a good idea?" she asked nervously.

"Mr Cooper is more influential than he was when you last saw him. If he doesn't like someone, he makes it very clear. It doesn't matter if you were a child; he will crush you if he wants." Byron swallowed. "And as you two are previously acquainted with Maurice, he isn't happy with the reunion. We don't want you to be hurt further."

"But where will we go?"

"We've got that sorted." Maurice led Polly to the gate and opened it. "We'll wait for you in the cart, Byron. We can't stay here."

"I'll be right there." Byron never took his eyes off Jennie. "Please, Jennie. You know this is the right thing to do. We can make sure you're safe and away from here, but you're going to have to come with us."

Jennie knew she should. She couldn't stay if Mr Cooper was going to discredit her. Her reputation, in her employer's eyes, had been ruined, and she wouldn't be able to protest any further. Her future as a teacher was gone.

This was her better option.

"Go, Jennie," Mr Davies said gently. "Your belongings are in the back of the cart. I've also written a letter of recommendation for your future position, so you don't have to worry about that."

"I...I don't know what to say."

"You don't need to say anything. You deserve better." Mr Davies sheepishly rubbed the back of his neck. "I never thought I'd be getting a soft spot for someone, but it happened. Now, are you going or not?"

Jennie stared at him. Then she hugged him around the waist. The schoolteacher made a sudden noise and stumbled. Then he was awkwardly patting her back.

"Off you go."

"Thank you, sir." Jennie looked up at him, feeling her eyes sting as tears began to build. "I appreciate what you've done for me. Thank you so much."

Mr Davies cleared his throat and nodded briskly. Then he

stepped away, giving Byron a nod, before walking back across the field. Byron took Jennie's hand and tugged.

"Come on. We haven't got long before our fathers wonder where we've gone."

He led her out of the field and helped her into the back of the cart. Maurice and Polly were sitting up front, Polly's shoulders hunched as she sobbed. Maurice hugged her tightly before reaching for the reins. He looked into the back as Byron and Jennie settled down.

"Ready to go?"

"Yes," Byron replied.

The cart started moving, Jennie looking at the bags tucked into the corner. That was all she and Polly had. They barely had any money, or any clothes. All Jennie had was books. Maybe she could sell them for some money if they couldn't get any further. It would be enough for clothes. She could buy more books eventually. Her focus was getting settled elsewhere.

"Why are you doing this?" she asked Byron, looking up at him. "Why are you helping us?"

Byron snorted.

"You think I wouldn't help you when you're in trouble? I'd be a terrible friend if I didn't do anything when you're going to be maligned for something you've never done."

"I know, but..."

"Maurice and I are not heartless, you know. If there's anything you and Polly need, we'll make sure you get it." Byron shuffled closer and put his arm around her, pulling her close. "You know we'll look after you."

"But aren't you going to get into trouble with your parents about this?" Jennie frowned at him. "What about then?"

Byron shook his head.

"We don't care about that. Our focus is you two." He kissed her forehead, letting his lips linger before he pulled back. "Don't worry about us, Jennie. Focus on yourself and getting what you want in life. That's more important."

Jennie was stunned by the fact he had just kissed her head. He had never done such an affectionate gesture before. She was left speechless, startled that he had even done that.

Then the gravity of the situation hit her. She was having to leave what she was used to and move into something new, something she didn't know. Nobody would tell her where they were going. Despite the warm evening weather, she felt incredibly cold.

She couldn't stop herself from shivering, and then the tears began to fall. Byron's arms tightened around her.

"Don't cry, Jennie. It's going to be all right. We'll make sure you're safe."

"I feel like you're doing too much for me, Byron."

Byron didn't immediately respond. Then he tilted her chin up and kissed her. Jennie was so surprised she barely realised what was going on. Byron pulled back and smiled at her, stroking her cheek.

"If anything, I don't feel like I'm doing enough," he said quietly. "I'll do anything for you, Jennie. You should know that by now."

"I..."

"Trust me, I'm not someone who can walk away from a person I care about. I'll do whatever I can to make you safe."

Jennie didn't know what to say to that. She was still stunned from the kiss. Byron had never been that affectionate with her before. She licked her lips and managed to find her voice.

"Thank you," she whispered. "I mean it."

Byron's smile warmed and he kissed her again, this time very briefly, before tucking her into his arms.

"I know," he said quietly.

CHAPTER 13

"How are the children getting on, Jennie?"

Jennie smiled at her mistress as she stood in the doorway of the schoolroom.

"They're doing very well. They've understood their sums very quickly."

Mrs Bartlett beamed.

"That's wonderful! I was beginning to despair at them not understanding anything. My last governess thought they were stupid."

"It was nothing. They just need a gentler hand to guide them, and then they can manage on their own." Jennie checked over the shoulder of Amanda Bartlett as she scribbled numbers down. "It seems to have worked."

"I suppose I should have told their last governess not to be so strict, but she insisted the children needed a firmer hand." Mrs Bartlett looked at the bowed heads of her son and daughter. "They're certainly happier now."

Jennie felt a swell of pride in her chest. She was glad that someone had noticed. It had been a month since she had arrived at Mrs Bartlett's home in St Albans, and things had improved.

She hadn't expected to become a governess to two young children with only one recommendation, but it had been enough that Mr and Mrs Bartlett agreed to take her in.

The bonus of having Polly as the children's nursery maid made things easier for the young family. Mr Bartlett was often in London working long hours, and Mrs Bartlett had been struggling to look after their children.

Knowing their contributions helped made Jennie feel better about herself.

"Anyway, do you mind if they come back to their lessons later?" Mrs Bartlett sighed heavily. "I've just received a message from my husband and his mother is coming for lunch. I know what she's like with time and she's always so early. If nobody's ready to receive her, she's going to be annoyed, and I don't want to deal with that."

"Do you want Polly and I to get the children ready, then?" Jennie asked.

"If you would, please."

Jennie nodded and began to shepherd Megan and James out of the room. She had encountered Mr Bartlett's mother before, and she was an incredibly abrasive woman. If something wasn't up to her very high standard she didn't hold back. Jennie was surprised at how outspoken she was, but she wasn't going to argue.

She was glad that she could escape and hide away when the woman visited as Mrs Bartlett would look after the children.

Polly was in the nursery tidying the toys when Jennie came in with Megan and James. She pointed towards their bedroom.

"I've already laid out your nicer clothes, children. Do you want some help with them?"

"No, we can do it." James took his sister's hand and lifted his chin defiantly. "We're not babies."

Polly smiled.

"I can see that. Well, why don't you two start and if you need any help, call for me."

The eight-year-old boy nodded and tugged his seven-year-old sister along with him, the door shutting behind them. Jennie shook her head with a smile.

"He acts far older than his age, doesn't he?"

"He's very mature. And he hasn't had to deal with our hardships." Polly sighed, continuing to tidy the toys away. "I wish I'd had something like that when I was eight. Things seem inconsequential at that age."

Jennie couldn't argue with that. She had been in the workhouse already at the age of eight, wishing for a better life. Right now, it seemed to be pretty good, but there was still that dark cloud on the horizon. She worried that she would see Mr Cooper barging into the house to tell Mrs Bartlett many untruths about her.

That had stopped her from relaxing completely. While Byron might have been able to secure a position for both of them through a friend of his at university - his older brother was looking for a governess - it didn't mean they were fully safe from repercussions. It had only been a month, but if Mr Cooper wanted to find them, he would.

She wandered over to the window and looked out into the gardens. It was green and lush with many beautiful flowers in full bloom. A gardener was cutting the grass, occasionally stopping to press his hands to his back as he stretched. They were on the outskirts of St Albans, so the days were mostly quiet with the occasional chirping from the birds.

Jennie found it surprisingly soothing not having to hear machinery all night, and she didn't have to wake up and work in a hot bakery all day. Two small children with sharp minds and quick wits was better than what she had before.

She thought about Byron and Maurice and wondered what they were doing. They promised to keep in touch, but the letters both her and Polly sent were going unanswered. There had been nothing from them for the last few weeks. Jennie was beginning to think they had put them elsewhere and decided to forget about them.

It was painful to know they might have been discarded, but Jennie couldn't dwell on it. They had been given a chance for something better, and they were going to have to make the most of it. At least their pay was better than before, and Jennie was doing something she loved.

"Do you think we'll hear from them soon?"

Jennie turned to Polly, who was closing the lid of the toybox. She looked downcast. Jennie attempted a smile.

"I'm sure we will. Their parents are going to be watching over them to make sure they're not in contact with us."

"I know, but...surely, they would have figured how to write back." Polly bit her lip. "Maurice promised me. He wouldn't break that."

Jennie approached her friend and hugged her. She could feel tears building, but refused to let them fall.

"It's going to be fine. Even if they never contact us again, we've been given a chance, and we're making the most of it." She stepped back. "I know you care about Maurice..."

"I love him, Jennie," Polly sniffed miserably. "He actually said he wanted to marry me, and he was going to make sure that happened."

"Really? He said that?"

Polly nodded. Jennie's heart cracked for her friend. Mr Cooper knew about that, and he would do everything in his power to make sure his son never followed through. As for Byron's parents...

She didn't want to think about it. It just made her feel sick thinking that they had been abandoned again. But she would not entertain those thoughts. Jennie managed a smile and squeezed her friend's hands.

"Well, if I know him, that's going to happen. You'll be married to Maurice and living your own life soon."

"I hope so." Polly peered at her. "Are you going to have the same with Byron? I know he's mad about you."

Jennie blinked.

"What? Mad on me?"

"He's in love with you. I noticed that years ago. I'm surprised you haven't."

Jennie was at a loss for words. She hadn't anticipated that at all. How was it possible that she had missed that? She couldn't believe that Byron loved her.

That would mean the feelings she had been carrying around for years weren't just unrequited. She could feel her head spinning.

"I...I didn't know."

Polly looked sympathetic.

"It's not something that he would have declared, though. He was scared you'd run away from him."

"Me? Run away from him?"

"Because you wouldn't want to have him ruin himself for you." Polly took Jennie's hands. "I know what you're like. If he had confessed his feelings, you would have panicked and told him he needed to find someone who his parents would approve of."

"But..."

"You know you would do that, Jennie."

Jennie faltered as the words sank in. With a growing realisation, she knew that Polly was right. If Byron had declared his love for her, it would have sent her into a state of shock. With their social standings, it wouldn't have been allowed. The scandal would have been incredibly shocking, and questions would have been raised about her moral standing. Jennie didn't want to go through any of that.

"I'm sorry, Jennie. I didn't mean to upset you."

"It's fine." Jennie wiped at a tear that escaped. She hadn't anticipated crying right now. "I guess I'm just feeling a little low because I haven't heard from Byron in a long time. He said he would write, and I've heard nothing."

"Maurice said the same. Maybe they've been caught."

"But what if they decided not to bother with us once we were out of sight?"

Before Polly could answer, the door to the bedroom opened and Megan and James came out. They were dressed in their smarter clothes, although the buttons on James' shirt and Megan's dress were a little crooked. Jennie smiled and approached them.

"That's not bad at all." She crouched before Megan. "Let's get those buttons in the right order, shall we?"

"Are you crying, Miss Clarke?" Megan asked.

"I'm fine, dear. I just got something in my eye." Jennie looked around when the sound of the bell rang through the house. "Sounds like your grandmother is here already. So that's good timing."

"I don't want to see Grandmother," James said, making a face. "She's not very nice."

"She's just very strict, that's all. Polly, would you mind getting a hairbrush from the dresser? We'll get their hair looking like they haven't been in a wind storm and adjust the buttons. Then they'll be ready."

"Can't we go through a hedge instead?" Megan said brightly. "That would be more fun than seeing Grandmother."

That made Jennie laugh. Megan was always coming out with things that took her by surprise. At least, even with everything still hanging over her, the future she had been given now was looking brighter.

If she could find her brother and see Byron again, then it would be considered perfect.

* * *

1870

Jennie hovered at the top of the stairs as Mrs Midgley, the housekeeper, received the letters from the postmaster. The blast of cold air shot through the hallway and up the staircase, causing Jennie to shiver. She loved the sight of snow, but she hated the cold itself.

She headed downstairs as Mrs Midgley shut the door.

"Who are they for, Mrs Midgley?"

"Most are for Mr Bartlett, a couple for Mrs Bartlett…" The housekeeper went through the letters. "That's it."

"Oh." Jennie deflated a little. "I see. Well…thank you, Mrs Midgley."

"Is something wrong, dear? Were you expecting something?"

Jennie shrugged, trying to sound nonchalant.

"I suppose. I don't know." She turned away. "I'll go and get the schoolroom ready. Megan and James will have finished with their breakfast."

She didn't want to explain it to the housekeeper. Mrs Midgley was a kindly woman, but a bit of a gossip. Jennie didn't want everyone in the household to know about her situation. She was already embarrassed that Mr and Mrs Bartlett were aware of what happened, even if it was a lot of malicious words.

She had been in their employ for six months now. She didn't want to have anything to change it.

As she wandered into the schoolroom, her fingers went to the pendant she had around her neck. It was on a piece of string, a red jewel set in pewter that settled against her throat. She could easily keep it under her collar without anyone raising questions about it.

There had been no note with the gift that had arrived for her a few days before Christmas just a couple of weeks ago, but Jennie was certain it was from Byron. She was aware that her birthstone was garnet, which was red, and Byron would know about that. Why he didn't send a note with it as well, she had no idea, but Jennie knew it was his present to her.

She had been tempted to send him something back, but if his parents saw it and guessed he was still in some sort of contact with her, it would be trouble for all of them.

If only she could see him again. She wanted to know that he was all right, that he hadn't forgotten about her. It left her with a hollow feeling in her stomach that she felt sick knowing that he might have moved on now she wasn't around. Jennie didn't want to think like that and believe Byron could do such a thing, but she couldn't stop the thoughts from floating around her head.

She missed him. She felt like there was an empty feeling inside her not having him around. Jennie hadn't anticipated that happening until she settled in with the Bartlett household. It was nice to be accepted and treated better than she had been at the two factories, but Byron wasn't there. It might have made things perfect if that had happened.

She pushed all thoughts of him out of her head. It was going to make things complicated for her if she wasn't careful. Jennie needed to focus and put her energy into looking after the children. She couldn't have any distractions.

"Oh, Jennie! There you are!" Mrs Bartlett entered the schoolroom ahead of her children, who went straight to their desks and sat down. She held out a letter. "This came for me, but it's regarding you."

"Me?" Jennie squeaked. Panic tightened in her stomach. "What is it about?"

"I thought you could tell me. Someone saying they're your brother Stephen and they're wondering if the governess I have is the same Jennie Clarke who is his older sister."

For a moment, Jennie thought she had misheard. A roaring started in her ears. This couldn't be happening, surely?

"Stephen?" She swayed. "Oh, my goodness."

"Careful!" Mrs Bartlett caught her and led her over to a nearby chair. "Sit down, dear."

"Is Miss Clarke all right?" James asked.

"I'm fine, James." Jennie managed a small smile. "I just…had a shock."

Frowning, Mrs Bartlett looked at the children and gestured towards the door.

"James, Megan, can you go and find Polly? I need a moment with Miss Clarke."

"But we just sat down…" James began, but a sharp look from his mother had him scurrying out of the room, Megan following behind. As the door closed, Mrs Bartlett turned back to Jennie.

"What is it? Do you know a Stephen?"

"Yes. Well, I used to." Jennie swallowed. "My little brother is Stephen. We were separated after our parents died. I haven't seen him in…fourteen years."

"Fourteen years?" Mrs Bartlett stared. "You were separated for that long? I'm surprised you weren't kept together."

"I don't know why, but we were. I've been trying to look for him for a long time, but nothing." Jennie looked at her hands, which were shaking. "If this is real…I can't believe it. Is it really my brother?"

"Well, he's asking for details about you to confirm that it's you." Mrs Bartlett held out the letter. "He gave a few examples that he said only you would know about to confirm it. And that if you are his sister, he wants to meet you with my permission."

Jennie felt like she couldn't breathe. She didn't know if she wanted to cry, faint, or scream. How was this happening now? It couldn't be possible. Even after paying someone to find Stephen, she had given up hope. Now he was alive and asking after her?

"I think you need a moment alone to gather your thoughts." Mrs Bartlett pressed the letter into Jennie's hands and stood up. "I'll get Polly to take the children out for their walk now so you can have some time alone. Let me know what you want to do."

"Thank you, Mrs Bartlett. I will do."

Her employer gave her a small smile before leaving the room, glancing back as she stepped out. As the door closed behind her, Jennie turned the letter over. If this was Stephen, and he was close by…

She felt like she was moving too fast. She needed to take a deep breath.

Her hands still shaking, she opened the letter and unfolded it. Then she began to read.

CHAPTER 14

It was him. Jennie couldn't believe it. Stephen was alive, and he wanted to see her. Apparently, he had been looking for her since he left the orphanage, but he had no idea where to look. It was only by luck he heard about her being so close by.

Now they were going to meet face-to-face for the first time in fourteen years. Jennie felt like she was living in a dream.

Mrs Bartlett was kind enough to let her use the morning room for their reunion, saying she would make sure nobody bothered them. Jennie couldn't thank her employer enough for doing everything for her. It was incredibly sweet, and Jennie felt like crying. Not for the first time, she was glad that Byron had taken her to the Bartlett household.

Maybe she should ask Mr Bartlett if he knew how to get a message to Byron. Jennie wanted to hear from him, just to know that he was all right. She missed him so much, and she couldn't think about being separated from him for much longer. If he had decided to move on, she wanted to hear from him first.

It would be enough for her to move forward as well. Even if it broke her heart.

"He's here!" Polly hissed, leaning against the window to see the visitor at the front door. "He's here!"

"Get away from the window before you hurt yourself, Polly. You'll knock your head on the glass."

"I won't..." Polly bumped her cheek against the pane and groaned. "Ouch!"

Jennie sighed.

"I told you. Anyway, why don't you go and let him in? Then you can stop hovering over me."

"I'm not hovering!"

"Polly..."

Polly huffed and dusted herself down.

"All right, fine! I just want to be sure you're safe, that's all. This is hard on you, isn't it?"

Jennie gave her friend a reassuring smile. She understood Polly's concern, but she was confident that nothing was going to happen. It would be fine for both of them, she was certain of it.

"You don't need to worry about me so much."

"That's easier said than done. I think I've been doing that for fourteen years." Polly headed towards the door as the bell rang. "I'll be right back."

She left the room, and Jennie found herself pacing around. She tried to sit down, but she couldn't. Her fingers hurt from twisting together until she almost bent them back on each other. Her heart was racing, and her nerves had been on edge since sending back a letter the day before.

This was her brother. For the first time, she was seeing him. How was she going to react? Did she rush at him and hug him immediately? Or did she wait and see how he behaved first? Jennie didn't want to make their reunion an embarrassing one.

She had been waiting for this moment for over a decade. Now it was happening, and it felt like she was going into hysterics.

The door opened, and Polly led a young man into the room. Jennie's breath lodged in her throat as she took in who was before her. He was taller than her and lean, hair the same colour as hers tousled on his head with a strong jaw and broad shoulders. He looked like he was slightly too big for his clothes.

He had been four years old when Jennie had last seen him. She had worried that she wouldn't recognise him. But she needn't have been concerned. He looked just like their father. It was like seeing a young version of their parent.

It was Stephen.

A noise made Jennie jump, and she realized that she was the one making the whimpering. She put her hands to her mouth, trying to stop herself, but it came out and she started to cry.

"Oh, my goodness."

"Jennie?" Stephen stepped towards her. "Is it really you?"

Jennie couldn't answer. She nodded, and then she rushed over to him. Stephen caught her as she flung her arms around his neck, and they embraced tightly. He was solid and warm, and Jennie could feel his heart racing against her chest.

He was here in front of her. Finally.

"I can't believe this." Jennie managed to pull back to stare up at him, cupping his face in her hands. "You look exactly like Pa."

"And you look just like Ma. I would have recognized you immediately." Stephen had a dazed look on his face. "How long have you been in St Albans?"

"About six months."

"I've been living here about a year now."

Jennie stared.

"What?"

"I work at the post office as an apprentice. I'm mostly sorting and delivering letters."

He was that close all this time and she hadn't known? Jennie felt her chest tightening, and she forced herself to breathe. As Polly shut the door, giving Jennie a nod with a smile, Jennie led her brother over to the settee and sat down heavily. Stephen sat beside her.

"What happened?" She stared at him. "How did you end up in St Albans? I thought you were in London?"

"I was until I was taken to a factory in Hitchin. Then I was picked out by the postmaster here to work for him."

"You were in Hitchin all this time?" Jennie felt like her head was spinning. "I was in Houghton for several years. I was only a couple of hours away. If I'd known…"

"There wasn't much we could have done. It's not as if they would have allowed us to see each other."

He had a point. Jennie looked at her hand clasped in his. His fingers were longer and warmer than hers, curled around hers. It was comforting. She felt like things were beginning to settle.

"I wanted you to come with me so much," she whispered. "I made Mr Cooper promise that you would come to me once you were old enough. But he didn't do that. He broke his promise."

"If I recall, he was the one who specifically made sure I didn't end up with you."

"What?"

Stephen nodded.

"I remember when I was sent to Hitchin asking if you were there, but I was told I would never see you again. It wasn't until I was a bit older that I found out it was on the instructions of a Mr Cooper to keep us apart."

"But why would he do that?"

"I have no idea. He's just a horrible man who tried to hurt you." Stephen peered at her. "He did hurt you, didn't he?"

Jennie didn't know how to answer that without blurting everything out. She nodded. Stephen squeezed her hands.

"I heard about it all. I felt awful that I wasn't there with you. I wished that I could've been there when you were going through all of that. Especially when he tried to ruin your reputation by talking badly about you."

"Wait a moment." Jennie frowned. "What are you talking about? How did you hear about that?"

Stephen blinked.

"You're not aware?"

"Of what?"

"Byron Harrison has been in contact with me."

Jennie thought she must have misheard. It took a moment for her mind to catch up to what her brother had just said. How did he know Byron's name? She was glad that she was sitting down, otherwise she might have collapsed.

"You…you know Byron? How?"

"He contacted me just after Christmas. Said that he had met my sister and knew where you were." Stephen shook his head in bewilderment. "I never expected you to be just up the road from me, though. That was a shock."

Jennie tried to get everything to sink in, but it didn't want to. Byron had contacted Stephen, and he knew where her brother was?

Why hadn't he told her about it?

"And…he told you everything?"

"Yes. Including how you hired someone to look for me. Apparently, you were given incorrect information about my location. It got mixed up with someone else I had been at the orphanage with." Stephen shrugged. "Although I wouldn't be surprised if someone told you something else to make you look in another direction."

Jennie swallowed. This felt like a lot to take in.

"I wouldn't be surprised. Mr Cooper would never follow through on his promise to bring us back together. I should have refused to go with him had I known he would do that."

"We were children. We trusted grownups to be truthful and look after us. And we learned the hard way that not everyone is like our parents." A shadow passed across Stephen's face. "I miss Ma and Pa. Every day, I think about them and how things might have been different if they were still alive, and we hadn't been separated as we were."

"I miss them, too," Jennie murmured. She could feel tears pricking at her eyes, and she blinked them away. She wasn't about to burst into tears in front of her brother, not when her emotions were overflowing again.

"It looks like we're doing all right for ourselves now, though," Stephen said, looking around the room. "You've got a good position, and you seem to have a kind employer."

"I do. Mr and Mrs Bartlett are so kind and generous. Byron…" Jennie felt odd saying his name after not hearing from him for so long. "He knew them, and he arranged for my friend and I to come here after trouble started back in Houghton. They knew our position and looked after us."

"And you like your life here now?"

"I do. It's the first time I've been truly treated kindly by everyone around me, not just a few select people. The children are adorable, I've got more freedom, and I'm treated like I'm part of the family. It's all I've ever wanted, to have a family."

Stephen smiled.

"And now you've got it," he said. "Even before I came back."

Jennie winced.

"That sounded awful, didn't it?"

"Not really. I completely understand. I've been living with my master since he brought me here to work for him, and he's an incredibly generous man. I couldn't continue my education beyond the age of eleven, so he's helping me catch up."

"I guess I was lucky with that. I had my lessons right until I had to leave the mill."

"Now I'm envious." Stephen squeezed her hands. "I can't believe we were so close to each other. I've even made deliveries to this house, and I never realised you lived here. So close and no yet I had no idea."

Jennie couldn't argue with that. She found it shocking they had been practically passing each other in the street and neither of them noticed.

She focused on a more pressing question.

"How long has Byron known that you're here? Did he really reach out to you at Christmas?"

"He did. I was stunned at first and thought it was a prank of some sort. But I wrote back out of curiosity, and soon he was turning up at the post office, telling me that you were close by, and I should see for myself. He was determined to bring us back together."

"But...why wouldn't he have contacted me? It's been six months since I last saw him, and I've heard nothing." Jennie tried not to shake as she fought back her emotions. "I would have thought he would tell me since it's all I've wanted to know since we were forced apart. I don't know why he would not tell me about this."

"He said that he wanted to do something for you as a present, a surprise, and he also didn't want to get your hopes up in case it wasn't me." Stephen chuckled. "When we talked in person, most of what he said about you was very glowing. I didn't need to ask if he was in love with you. It was obvious to see how he felt about you."

"I...I..." Jennie stuttered.

"You've got a good man there, Jennie. I'm very impressed you got someone like Byron looking out for you. I'm also surprised that you're not married by now, seeing as I'm sure that would have happened already if circumstances hadn't got in the way."

Jennie didn't know what to say to that. She sank back against the cushions and closed her eyes, but that didn't stop her pounding headache.

"This is too much to take in," she said.

"I understand. You've just met me again, and Byron is waiting to hear from you..."

"Where is he now?"

Stephen hesitated, glancing towards the door.

"He said he was going to speak to Mrs Bartlett while I was in here talking to you. He's probably somewhere in the house right now waiting for us to catch up."

Byron was here right now. Jennie's heart raced. For the first time in months, he was close enough for her to see him. She felt lightheaded and was glad she was sitting down.

"You should go to him," Stephen whispered.

"And what about you?"

Her brother chuckled.

"It's been fourteen years since I lost you, Jennie. We've got the rest of our lives to catch up. But men like Byron Harrison don't come along often. I think you should go see him."

Jennie didn't need to be told twice. But after she stood up, she leaned over and hugged him tightly.

"I love you, little brother," she said, kissing his cheek.

"And I love you, big sister." Stephen smiled and jerked his head towards the door. "Go. He's waiting for you."

* * *

POLLY WAS HOVERING around in the hall when Jennie hurried out. Her eyes were bright, and she looked excited.

"They're here!" she cried.

"They?" Jennie frowned. "Who are you talking about?"

"Byron and Maurice! They're both here!"

"Maurice as well?"

Polly nodded, her expression showing her delight. She grasped Jennie's hands, practically jumping up and down.

"Mrs Bartlett put them in the dining room. I've already seen Maurice, so we're going for a walk shortly. But Byron wants to see you."

Jennie wasn't about to delay it. She hurried to the dining room and entered. Maurice and Byron were sitting at the table, and both got to their feet when she came in. Jennie was shocked to see both, but her gaze was focused on Byron.

He looked like he had grown in the last few months, or maybe that was her imagination. He was dressed very smartly, accentuating his broad shoulders and chest. He looked like he hadn't shaved in a few days, but it showed off his strong-looking jaw.

How had the person she had known for years suddenly grown up in the short time they were apart?

They stared at each other, both seeming unable to move. Then Byron strode towards her. Jennie couldn't move, but she clutched onto Byron as he embraced her, holding onto her tightly as if he expected her to be a mirage. He buried his face into her neck and let out a heavy sigh of relief.

"Thank God," he rasped. "Thank God."

Jennie wondered what he meant by that. She pulled back and looked up at him, touching his face as if unsure that it was really him. He was solid under her fingertips, and he smiled as she did that.

"I'm really here," he said. "And I'm not going anywhere."

"You'd better not," Jennie shot back with a smile. "I don't want to be abandoned like that again."

"I'm so sorry I had to do that to you."

"We didn't have a choice with our parents," Maurice added. Jennie had momentarily forgotten he was in the room. "They were keeping a close eye on us and reading our letters. After the first letters from you and Polly, they forbid us from sending anything at all. We couldn't even sneak anything out."

"They were that strict on you despite being grown men?"

Maurice shrugged.

"Unless we marry and get our own households, we must have our parents watching over us. It's frustrating, but we couldn't do much."

"We were lucky enough that I was able to communicate with the man you hired to find your brother," Byron said. "Through Mr Davies, I managed to get in contact with him and got him to communicate through the schoolteacher if he found anything about your brother. It took some time, but he found him. And you can imagine my shock when I found out he was only a stone's throw away from your new home."

Jennie slapped his arm.

"And you didn't think to tell me? You could have used Mr Davies!"

"I wanted a surprise for you. And if the information was wrong, I didn't want you to get your hopes crushed."

That was understandable, but Jennie wished she had been told. It would mean she had some communication with Byron. She licked her lips.

"I thought you had turned your back on me," she whispered. "I thought you didn't care about us anymore."

Byron didn't say anything for a moment. He glanced at Maurice and nodded. His friend cleared his throat and headed towards the door, pausing to squeeze Jennie's shoulder before he left. Byron growled as the door shut.

"I was beginning to think he would never leave."

Jennie squeaked as he kissed her, cupping her head in his hands. Then she gripped onto his shoulders, sinking into his embrace as the kiss deepened. Her head was spinning when they stopped, both breathing heavily. Byron groaned, resting his forehead against hers.

"You have no idea how long I've wanted to do that."

"I've missed you."

Jennie couldn't hold it in. She just found herself blurting out. Byron smiled and kissed her forehead.

"And I've missed you. I wanted to defy my parents and come after you, to get you to come home and be with me. But they were adamant that I would not have any contact with you."

"Yet you're here now. Does that mean you don't care anymore?"

Byron's smile faded a little. He took her hands, linking his fingers with hers. It was something they often did as children, and Jennie found some comfort in it.

"This surprise with your brother would have happened either way, but things have…changed at home."

"What do you mean by that?"

"Mother…she had a stroke."

Jennie's mouth dropped open.

"Oh my. She had a stroke? But she's only in her forties! I thought strokes were for older people."

Byron grunted.

"So did I. But they can affect anyone and come out of nowhere. It happened in November, and Father's been doing everything to look after her. But in focusing on her, he's not paying attention to the mill, and he's torn with his responsibilities. When I got confirmation from Stephen's letter that he really was your brother, I sat him down and offered to take over the mill for him."

"You did?"

He nodded.

"Father knows I have some ideas for the mill, some of which he wasn't in agreement with, so he was still reluctant about it. He's been in charge for years, after all, and it's what keeps his family going. But I pointed out Mother was more important to him, and he needed to focus on her. I can take care of everything else." He paused. "Also, it would stop Mr Cooper from taking over. He had been pushing to be put in charge for weeks before this talk, but Father was refusing as he thought he could handle it all. And, if I'm honest, he wanted to keep it in the family."

Jennie shuddered. Mr Cooper didn't deserve to oversee anything. The mill wasn't much better than the factory she had been in before, but the conditions were slightly improved. If Mr Cooper took charge, he would have ruined everything.

"So, did he agree to it?" she asked.

"He did. He said that I was old enough to be in charge, and he knew I wouldn't do anything to affect productivity." Byron smiled. "He even said he would give his blessing if I could prove that I can handle everything."

"For what?"

"To have you as my wife."

Jennie wondered if there was a part of the conversation that she had missed. She tried to get the words back in order, but there was nothing.

"What did you just say? He gave his blessing for me to be your wife?"

"I know, I was surprised when he said that as well, especially when he had been so adamant about me not ruining the family reputation for so long." Byron's fingers ran over the back of her knuckles. "But he said he had seen me so miserable the last few months and knew it was because I couldn't see you. He didn't want me to be upset, but the only way to make me happy was to say I could see you again. Things changed when Mother…tried to match me with someone."

"Pardon me?" Jennie squeaked.

"She said I needed to marry and start a family, and she attempted to match me with the daughter of a friend. But that fell through, mostly because the friend's daughter was courting someone herself, someone they didn't approve of."

Jennie couldn't help but giggle at that.

"That must have been an interesting conversation."

"More than interesting, and it would have been amusing if I hadn't been a part of it. I argued with Mother about that, telling her that I didn't want anyone as my wife unless it was you. She had a stroke a couple of weeks later, and with a threat to her health and trying to recover, she began to see that getting me to do something I don't want isn't worth the effort. Of course, she and Father still have reservations due to society norms and how it's going to look, but they would rather me be happy around them than miserable."

Jennie let all that sink in, but it felt like some of the words were refusing to go in. She shook her head, but that didn't do any good.

"So, you're saying that you want to marry me? Because…"

"Isn't it obvious by now, Jennie? I love you. I always have." Byron leaned in and kissed her, drawing it out slowly before he pulled back. "Being away from you was difficult. I didn't think I'd be able to cope at all, so seeing you is making my decision final. I don't want to be apart from you for any longer. I love you too much to let you walk away."

Jennie stared at him, his expression earnest. She had been hoping for words like this before, although her hope had ebbed away in recent months. Now she was hearing what she had dreamed of, and it was making her heart flutter. She couldn't stop herself from smiling, grabbing his head and kissing him herself. Byron looked amused when they came up for air.

"I have a feeling I've got my answer to how you feel."

"You can't imagine how hard it was to not hear from you for months, Byron, but I never stopped loving you." Jennie gripped his shoulders, half-expecting him to suddenly vanish. "I wanted you here with me, to make things better. But you weren't."

"I'm so sorry about that. I wish I could have stayed."

"Now you're here, I have no intention of letting you walk away." Jennie took a deep breath. "I know that sounds possessive, but after what we've been through recently…"

"I am not going to blame you for that at all. I've been feeling the same way." Byron put his arms around her and hugged her. "Although I think we should move out of this room before Mrs Bartlett comes in and sees us. She said she would give us five minutes alone, but that's the most I'm getting without pushing boundaries."

Jennie laughed.

"She doesn't know us that well, does she, if she thinks we can't get into trouble in five minutes."

Byron grinned, kissing her before getting to his feet, tugging Jennie upright.

"I think she would regret it if we told her of the escapades we did as children. But maybe we should go and find her to assure her things are going to be fine. Although she might be losing a governess soon if you're coming back with me."

"One thing at a time, Byron." Jennie squeezed his hand. "I think we've got plenty of time."

CHAPTER 15

1871

Jennie looked into the schoolroom and saw the children working in silence, their heads bent. She could have heard a pin drop with the quiet. Mr Davies sat at the front of the room reading a book and occasionally glancing up at the room. He caught sight of Jennie and gave her a nod with a slight smile. Jennie smiled back and withdrew.

She had a lighter skip in her step as she left the schoolhouse, which had recently been extended to have a few more rooms. Ever since she returned and made changes to improve the school and keep the children in education longer, things were flourishing. Even Mr Davies was surprised at how things were coming along. He found it a bit of a struggle to have Jennie in charge when she returned, but they had fallen into an easy partnership. The man understood her thoughts and ideas, which made it easier for both of them.

At least the children were looking happier. Jennie was surprised at how many children wanted to do something that wasn't working all day. They even got some time to just play. Of course they had a few hours still in the mill, but with the added employees and workers Byron had added in the last eighteen months, they weren't needed as much.

She went back to the house, heading into the garden. Stephen and Byron were sitting in chairs on the grass, enjoying the sun. Her brother saw her first and grinned.

"Big sister."

"Stephen!" Jennie beamed and hugged him as he got to his feet. "I thought you weren't coming until tomorrow."

"I decided to come a day earlier to surprise you." Stephen stared at her swollen belly. "Now I think you've surprised me as well."

Jennie laughed.

"I told you I was having a baby, didn't I?"

"You did, but I wasn't expecting it to be so…big. Are you sure you're not having twins or something?"

Byron groaned.

"Don't. Father asked me about that."

"And I would rather not have twins if I'm the one giving birth," Jennie added with a shudder. She sat in the chair Stephen had vacated, her brother placing a blanket across her lap. "The children are getting along fine with their lessons. Mr Davies doesn't need me hovering around."

"And the mill is doing well without me needing to stand over them, so I've left the foremen to it." Byron held up a letter that was in his lap. "This came from Maurice and Polly, by the way."

"All the way from Scotland?"

"They're having a grand time, although Maurice is worried that Polly might want to stay. She's looking forward to seeing you and the baby once she returns from their honeymoon." Byron smiled. "Mother also said she would like us to visit soon after the baby is born. Once you've rested, of course, but she would love to see us. Father tells me that she's been giddy ever since finding out we're having a child."

Jennie was happy about that. The woman who had suffered

from a stroke had become softer in her approach, and she and Jennie got along well. Byron's parents had moved to the Lake District for his mother's health, so it was a bit of a journey for either party, but they were certainly happier and more relaxed, from what they could guess in their letters. With Byron running the mill and Jennie focusing on the children, there was less for them to worry about.

"Do you think you're going to have a boy or a girl?" Stephen asked, sitting on the blanket by the chairs, stretching out his legs. "I would like a nephew."

"You don't want a niece?"

"I prefer little boys. They're a lot more fun."

Byron laughed.

"You should have seen Jennie and Polly as children. They were definitely not boring children."

Stephen shrugged.

"I suppose I won't mind either way, but I would like a nephew first."

"You'll have a niece or nephew to spoil either way," Jennie said, affectionately tapping her brother on the head. "Although I'm scared at how close I am to having this baby. I feel like I've been pregnant forever."

"It's going to be over soon." Byron reached over and took her hand. "We'll have our first child soon. Things are coming together nicely."

Jennie couldn't agree more. They had married soon after returning from St Albans and getting blessings from Byron's parents, right before she and Mr Davies began to work on the schoolhouse and Byron concentrated on the mill. Mr Cooper, who had been hovering in the wings, had been furious and tried to get in the way, but Byron dismissed him from the board and gave his shares to the other board members.

He said he wasn't willing to have someone who tormented his wife involved, and Mr Cooper was kicked out with much protest.

Maurice had told them he wished he had witnessed it because it would have been so sweet to watch his father being taken down a few pegs.

"It's hard to imagine this is our life now," Jennie said to Stephen, looking over the garden in full bloom, the river in the distance. "Not too long ago, you and I were being taken to an orphanage and split up. It's surprising how things worked out to get us back together."

"And now we're starting off in our own way." Stephen regarded her thoughtfully. "Do you think our parents would be proud of us and where we are now?"

Jennie looked over at Byron, who smiled and raised her hand to his mouth, kissing her knuckles. Her heart fluttered at the sight of him doing that. They hadn't been married long, and she didn't think she could be any happier. She rested a hand on her belly and felt the baby kick against her palm.

"I think they would be very proud of us," she said. "They would be happy. Especially now we're back together."

She wondered what Byron would say if they named their child after one of her parents. But, given how Byron happily gave her anything she asked, even if she was selective in what she asked, he would agree with her idea.

It would make a picture-perfect scene that had been so far out of her grasp years for years.

The End

If you enjoyed this story, could I please ask you to leave a review on Amazon?

Thank you so much.